DUELING WITH GIANTS

# DUELING WITH GIANTS

## BOOK I OF THE TALES OF ASGARD TRILOGY

## KEITH R.A. DE CANDIDO

**JOE BOOKS LTD**

Published simultaneously in the United States and Canada
by Joe Books Ltd, 567 Queen St. West, Toronto, ON M5V 2B6

*www.joebooks.com*

Library and Archives Canada Cataloguing in Publication
information is available upon request.

ISBN 978-1-77275-197-0 (print)
ISBN 978-1-98803-230-6 (ebook)

First Joe Books Edition: January 2016
3 5 7 9 10 8 6 4 2 1

Joe Books™ is a trademark of Joe Books Ltd.
Joe Books® and the Joe Books logo are trademarks of Joe Books Ltd,
registered in various categories and countries. All rights reserved.

Printed and bound in Canada

*Dedicated to the memory of Scooter (1999-2015), the best dog in the history of the world. We really miss you, you big galoot . . .*

# PRELUDE

The skies are sometimes blue, sometimes black, sometimes gray.

When storms come and go on Midgard—which its natives generally call "Terra" or "Earth"—and are followed by sunlight, the sky goes from gray to blue, and the people, if they look up at the right time, are blessed with the sight of a rainbow.

Scientists and teachers will explain that a rainbow is a result of the refraction of the sun's light through the moisture still left in the air from the storm. And while they are right, there is more to it than that.

If humans see a rainbow, then they are getting the briefest look at a much greater tapestry, for they have seen a glimpse of the Bifrost—the rainbow bridge that leads to Asgard.

Asgard and Midgard are but two of the worlds that are linked by Yggdrasil, the great world tree that connects the Nine Worlds to each other.

The lives of the natives of Midgard are but brief, over in an instant. The denizens of Asgard are far longer-lived, and much stronger and more powerful, controlling forces far beyond those of most mortals.

Today, some Asgardians do cross the Bifrost to Midgard,

where they are viewed as "paranormals" or "super heroes"—or, in some cases, "super villains." In this modern age, they are far from the only beings of power who walk Midgard's lands.

A thousand years ago, Asgardians crossed the Bifrost in greater numbers. The peoples of one particular region—some mortals call it "Scandinavia"—did view the Asgardians as gods, and paid them tribute, worshipping them and telling tales of their adventures.

And a thousand years before that, many of those who would be worshipped as gods in adulthood were still children.

On one such day, a blond-haired youth named Thor—the son of Odin, the ruler of Asgard—did approach the Bifrost. A young man named Heimdall had recently been appointed to be the guardian of the rainbow bridge, for his senses were more acute than any other in Asgard. He could see an army gathering from many leagues away, hear their approach, even smell the ointments they used to clean their swords and polish their armor.

And so he had no trouble detecting the approach of young Thor. The boy was carrying a sword and shield and had an eager and happy expression on his face.

"Heimdall!" he cried. "I have heard that the forces of evil will soon attack Asgard!"

"Yes," Heimdall said. "Odin's noble ravens, Hugin and Munin, have reported that there are rumblings of an alliance among many of the foes of Asgard. The Norn Hag, the Rime Giants, the trolls, and the wolf gods are joining forces to do together what they could never accomplish while apart."

Holding up his sword, Thor spoke solemnly. "Then I must defend the Realm Eternal! I am Odin's eldest son, and it is my duty!" Then his face broke into a grin. "Besides, if I do enough good deeds I will earn Odin's uru hammer!"

Heimdall smiled indulgently at the boy. He knew that his younger sister, Sif, thought highly of the lad, and Sif was not one to give her affections to someone unworthy.

But after a moment, Heimdall let his smile fall away, for he had only recently been appointed to this sacred duty. He would not allow Thor to distract him. "Go away, Thor. Rest assured, if any do attack Asgard, I will know it and I will sound the Gjallarhorn."

"And I will be ready by your side when—"

"If you are by my side, you will distract me from my post—as, indeed, you already are." He put a friendly hand on the youth's shoulder. "Go, return to your home. The Gjallarhorn will be heard throughout Asgard, should the rumors be true. When that happens, you may answer the call to arms with everyone else."

Despondent, Thor returned to his home. Odin, of course, was not there—he was always busy in the throne room with affairs of state—but his mother, Frigga, was present.

As always, Thor's mother knew his mood instantly. "What distresses you, my son?" she asked upon his entry.

"I tried to stand by Heimdall at the Bifrost, but he sent me away! I will never earn possession of Father's hammer if I do not perform noble deeds in the service of Asgard!"

"And is that the reason for your desire to stand by the Bifrost, my son?"

Thor frowned. "What do you mean?"

"I simply question whether or not your eagerness to defend the realm comes from a desire to protect the people of Asgard, or because of the trinkets you will be rewarded with if you do."

That brought Thor up short. "But—" He hesitated. "If I am granted Mjolnir, then I will be able to perform my duties more properly!" He held up his sword and shield. "These weapons are strong and true, but compared to Mjolnir they are no better than the wooden training weapons I used as a boy!"

Refraining from pointing out that Thor was *still* a boy, Frigga called her son to her. He placed his sword and shield upon the end table, and then sat next to her on the couch in the grand sitting room of their home. "So you wish a more powerful weapon?"

"Only that I may protect the people better! I may be the ruler of Asgard sometime in the future—should, the fates forfend, something happen to Father . . ."

"Yes," Frigga said quickly, not wishing to dwell on such a possibility. "But in that instance you will rule, not fight."

"But I *must* know that I can protect the people of Asgard as best I can. So I *must* have the hammer!"

"What if you *don't* have the hammer?"

"If I am not considered worthy of Mjolnir, then I am not fit to be Asgard's protector!"

Frigga smiled. "You need not worry, my son. You do not wish

Mjolnir for its own sake, but for its ability to allow you to serve your function greater. *That* is why I am sure you will be granted it—and also why you need not worry about *when* you will be worthy. Your intentions are pure, and all else will derive from that."

Thor smiled at his mother and suddenly leaned over and gave her a huge hug. "Thank you, Mother."

"Now shoo, and leave me in peace."

After retrieving his sword and shield from the end table, Thor said, "Of course, Mother. Again, thank you!"

Thor went toward the rear entrance of the house with a spring in his step. He would use the time practicing with his sword while he waited for Heimdall to sound the Gjallarhorn to signal the coming battle.

As he worked on his parries and his thrusts, Loki suddenly appeared as if from nowhere, startling Thor.

"You would be wise, my brother, not to be so stealthy when approaching one carrying a blade. I would not wish to hurt you by accident—or, indeed, on purpose."

Thor spoke the words with a truly sincere smile, for though Loki was not his blood, he was still kin in all the ways that mattered. Thor had nothing but affection for his brother.

Loki returned the sentiment with a smile that was far from sincere, for he did not share the good feelings of his adoptive brother. He had his own designs on Mjolnir, knowing it would be a valuable tool in his growing ability with spellcraft. But he knew that Thor was going to be the one to get it, barring a catastrophe.

And Loki was definitely the person to provide that catastrophe.

"Mother said you were back here, Thor. I heard that you were trying to find a way to perform good deeds, that our dear father may deem you worthy of his bequeathing Mjolnir upon you."

"Indeed! Heimdall tells me that many of Asgard's greatest foes are gathering and will invade soon. But Heimdall stands true at the rainbow bridge, and he will alert all Asgard when the attack comes."

"Assuming it comes to a place Heimdall can see."

Thor frowned. "What do you mean?"

"I have discovered something. Come with me!" Without even waiting to see if Thor followed, Loki ran back toward the house.

Of course, Thor did follow him. He was compelled to learn what his brother had found.

Loki led him down the spiral stairs to the catacombs, the tunnels that connected this, Odin's home, with the throne room, allowing the All-Father to traverse between his home and his place of rule in relative peace and quiet. After all, if Odin were to stride through the streets of Asgard, he would be a figure of admiration and gawking, and after a long day of responsibility, he wished to be on his way to his dwelling with dispatch.

Thor and Loki had both made use of these tunnels as well, but now Loki was leading Thor down a route he had never gone before.

"I had no idea the catacombs extended so far," Thor said.

"Indeed," was all Loki would say in reply.

The tunnels twisted and turned so many times that soon Thor had completely lost his way. Loki, however, remained sure of foot as he traversed the halls, finally arriving upon a bend.

Thor was surprised to feel a breeze, and when they came 'round the bend, he understood why: there was a great hole in the wall, which led to a grassy plain outside the city walls of Asgard.

"What perfidy is this?" Thor asked, aghast.

Loki smiled. "A quite literal hole in Asgard's defenses. It was mere happenstance that I came upon it while exploring these tunnels. It is possible that Heimdall will still see the hordes coming, but he may not. And if Asgard's foes come through here . . ."

Thor nodded, raising his sword. "You were wise to bring me here, Loki. I will stand fast at this breach and defend Asgard against those who would destroy her."

"Excellent!" Loki clapped Thor on the back. "I knew I could count on you. I will go and fetch assistance."

Loki very carefully waited until he was well out of Thor's earshot before bursting into laughter. The truth was, of course, that he had not so much come upon the hole while exploring the tunnels; rather he was the one who created the hole during those explorations. What's more, he had sent a message to Skoll and Hati, the wolf gods who had brought several of Asgard's greatest foes together to plan an assault. Loki had learned of their secret covenant by his own means, and was determined to help them succeed in their plan to attack—so that Loki himself could drive them away and earn Mjolnir for himself!

But first, he'd need to be rid of his tiresome brother. Mother may have been equal in her affections to them both, but Odin very obviously preferred the blond idiot. Loki would need to make sure that the wolf gods and their allies did their part and took Thor out before Loki could make his own move.

Sure enough, Thor soon found himself face to face with a most impressive collection of foes: the Norn Hag astride Ulfrin the Dragon, accompanied by the wolf gods, and several trolls and Rime Giants.

Never before in his young life had Thor seen so many foes come at him at once. And Loki had not yet returned with the promised reinforcements.

Faced with no alternative, Thor charged forward. Knowing he could not overwhelm so great a force with his strength alone, he instead used his blade to smash a nearby rock that he knew covered a hot spring. The heated water burst forth and knocked the wolf gods aside.

However, those who felt the enchanted breath of Ulfrin the Dragon rarely lived long to speak of it. At the Norn Hag's command, Ulfrin breathed a sickly green smoke that caused Thor's very limbs to grow weak. He dropped his sword, unable to even muster the strength to hold it, much less lift the weapon.

And then he remembered what he had said to Frigga about his duty to Asgard, and how he longed to be worthy of Mjolnir so he could keep Asgard safe.

Shaking off the effects of the dragon's breath, he reached for his sword and struck the beast in the gullet with a mighty blow.

The dragon thrashed in pain, throwing the Norn Hag from its back.

That left only the Rime Giants and the trolls, and soon Thor was fighting them all for his life, as they came at him from all sides.

Just as he believed he would be overwhelmed, just as he was sure that he would die protecting Asgard and be brought to Valhalla far sooner than he'd hoped, he heard a very familiar voice cry out, "For Asgard!"

Looking back, Thor saw that Odin had arrived, with a dozen more warriors by his side.

Within moments, the foes had retreated, unwilling to face so great a foe as Odin, much less his warriors, pledged to die defending him. They had hoped for the element of surprise when Loki came to them with his plan, and now that was lost. The water-soaked wolf gods, the wounded dragon, the humiliated Norn Hag, and the defeated giants and trolls beat a hasty retreat.

Thor knelt down before Odin. "I am sorry, Father, I failed to defend the Realm Eternal."

"I say nay, my son, rise to your feet." Odin smiled beneath his thick white beard. "Heimdall heard the sounds of battle from your sword against the rock, the dragon, and the creatures' weapons and he had us come. You did well—had you not been here to defend this opening, these brigands would have been well within Asgard's borders before we were able to muster a defense."

"It is not just I who should be thanked, Father. 'Twas Loki who brought me to this opening and bade me defend it while he summoned help."

"Did he, now?" Odin shook his head. "I shall have to make sure that Loki receives *all* due credit for his actions this day, then."

Thor went home that night with a happy heart, for he knew he was that much closer to earning Mjolnir.

For his part, Loki's heart was far less happy. His plan had completely failed, and he was upbraided by Odin for not fulfilling his promise to Thor to send for help. Loki pleaded innocent, saying he got lost in the tunnels, but Odin did not appear to believe him.

Despondent, Loki returned home. Frigga was present.

As with Thor, Loki's mother knew his mood instantly. "What distresses you, my son?" she asked upon his entry.

"I had hoped to stop the vanguard of enemies that attacked Asgard today—after they defeated Thor. Then Odin would see that *I* am the one who should wield Mjolnir!"

"You wished Thor to be harmed?"

"Well, perhaps a little," Loki admitted. "I just wanted him defeated so I could show Father that *I* am just as worthy a son as Thor."

"You *are* just as worthy a son, Loki. Remember, Odin *chose* you as his son. He did not do that lightly."

"Perhaps." Loki sat next to Frigga on the couch and folded his arms. "But why does he not see what I can contribute?"

"Because you attempt to show him only through paltry schemes and misdirection! And by endangering your brother, his *other* son. That is *not* the way to Odin's favor."

"Of course, you are correct, Mother. My schemes must be *brilliant!*"

"Loki—"

Rising from the couch, Loki quickly ran from the room. "Thank you, Mother!"

Frigga sighed. No one had said that raising two boys to become heirs to the throne of Asgard would be easy . . .

# CHAPTER ONE

When the troll's fist collided with Thor's head, the thunder god was at once surprised, exhilarated, and angered.

The surprise had been ongoing, commencing when the gaggle of trolls first appeared amongst Asgard's gleaming spires. Thor knew not how or why the creatures contrived to invade the home of the gods, but he had pledged long ago to protect the Realm Eternal at all costs. He did so two millennia ago when Loki led him to a hole in the tunnels beneath the city, and he did so now, and no doubt he would do so two millennia hence. Never would Thor shirk his duty to the Realm Eternal. And so from the very moment Heimdall sighted the trolls' invasion with his great vision, Thor took up Mjolnir and joined the fray. There would be time enough to learn the how and why of the incursion by the trolls after the battle was done. Indeed, such an investigation would need to take place, for Heimdall's all-seeing eyes should have detected the trolls' approach long before they got within Asgard's gates.

The exhilaration came from knowing he did not fight alone. His comrades-in-arms were right beside him: Balder the brave, Fandral the dashing, Hogun the grim, Volstagg the voluminous, and the mightiest of shield-maidens, the Lady

13

Sif. They were the doughtiest warriors a god could ask for to stand by his side, and Thor considered himself fortunate to number them among his friends as well as his battle-mates. Balder, Sif, and the Warriors Three had joined Thor in the square outside the Temple of Titans to face the thirteen trolls who had invaded the city.

The anger derived from the troll who had managed to sneak under Thor's guard and strike him. His winged helmet flew from atop his head, clanging to the ground beside him, and he also lost his grip on Mjolnir as he fell to the paving stones in a heap.

Thor looked up at the troll who had struck him, and smiled. "Well struck, but you will rue the day you challenged the son of Odin!"

Cackling in response, the troll said, "No such thing do I rue, thunderer, save that you still draw breath. I shall remedy that state of affairs now."

With that, the orange-skinned creature leapt at Thor's prone form. Thor raised his arms to defend himself from the troll's onslaught. Thor's foe was the biggest of the thirteen trolls who had invaded, standing head and shoulders above even Volstagg, the largest of the Asgardians. Doubtless that troll was the leader of the campaign, and Thor intended to defeat him directly. When he fell, the other dozen would soon follow.

The troll's meaty hands attempted to wrap around Thor's neck, and the thunder god countered by grabbing the creature's wrists. Though he could not break the troll's grip, Thor was able to keep his foe from impeding his ability to breathe.

Thor had once met an old god named Tiwaz, who nursed Thor back to health after a particularly nasty battle against the goddess of death, Hela. Part of the healing process had been that Thor had to wrestle Tiwaz each night in order to earn his supper. Wrestling had never been a significant component of the thunderer's combat arsenal in the past, but he learned a great deal from Tiwaz.

Today he put one of those lessons to good use. Though the troll was on top of him, Thor was able to use his hips to shift his weight back and forth, destabilizing the troll.

Soon, the pair was tumbling across the square, rolling toward the monument to Yggdrasil. The monument was a miniature re-creation of the ash that bound the Nine Worlds together, and Thor and the troll both crashed into it with a bone-jarring impact.

Their respective grips broken by their violent encounter with the monument, both Thor and the troll were momentarily dazed. Shaking it off, Thor clambered to his feet, pausing only for a breath to see how fared his comrades.

Balder was easily holding two of the trolls at bay with his sword, and a third lay at the shining one's feet.

Not to be outdone, Sif had left two troll corpses in her wake, and she was driving a third back toward the Temple of Titans with her blade.

Both Fandral and Hogun were holding their own with sword and mace, respectively, against two trolls each.

While trying to espy the last two trolls, Thor saw Volstagg sitting on the steps that led to the Temple of Titans, discoursing at great length. At first, Thor feared that the voluminous one had chosen to sit out the battle, but it soon became clear that sitting *was* the battle. The remaining pair of trolls were currently pinned to the temple stairs by Volstagg's rather large bottom. Said stairs were too distant for Thor to hear Volstagg's words, but no doubt the Lion of Asgard—who was one of the finest storytellers extant—was regaling the trolls with exaggerated tales of his exploits. Thor fully expected the trolls to admit defeat simply in a fruitless effort to get Volstagg to silence himself.

Satisfied that his friends were holding their own—and then some—Thor turned his attention back to the leader of the trolls. While they were all charged with the protection of Asgard, as the son of Odin and the heir to Asgard's golden throne, he had always felt the responsibility of keeping Asgard safe most keenly.

Which was why he had taken it upon himself to engage the trolls' leader. Cut off the head, and the body soon fell. Trolls in particular were a dim lot, and few had even a modicum of leadership skills. Thor knew that defeating this one would send the others into a tizzy.

And that was his responsibility as Asgard's protector. He would not allow these trolls to succeed where so many others had failed. Not while he drew breath, and not while he wielded Mjolnir.

"You are truly mighty, troll, and the thunder god salutes your effrontery. It is a true act of gall to invade the city of Asgard when all its defenders are near at hand. You risk much—but defeat will be your sole reward."

With that, Thor held up his hand and summoned Mjolnir to him.

Centuries ago, Odin approached Eitri, master of the dwarven smithies, and commissioned him to create a hammer from the enchanted metal uru that would become the mightiest weapon in the Nine Worlds. Molded from the core of an exploding star, tempered in the fires of the dwarves' forge, and infused with the enchantment of the All-Father himself, Odin named the resultant hammer Mjolnir, which means "that which smashes." Odin himself used it to defeat the giant Laufey. He had told his young son Thor that he would bequeath it to him if he were worthy, and Thor had spent considerable effort to make himself thus. The day Odin had at last gifted him with the hammer was the proudest of his long life.

Since that fateful day, Mjolnir had been as much a part of Thor as one of his limbs. Odin's enchantment meant that none but Thor could wield the hammer. Always when it flew from his grasp, it unerringly returned to him.

Until today. For Thor stood at the base of the monument to Yggdrasil, his hand outstretched—but Mjolnir remained on the ground of the square, unmoving.

The troll threw his massive head back and laughed. "Is the thunder god still truly that if he has not his great hammer? To mulch I'll pound you, Odinson, for without your hammer you're just another little god."

"I have heard such boasts from trolls since your kind first emerged from the caves whence you dwell, and never have I yielded."

"First time for everything," the troll muttered, and then again leapt at Thor.

The time for words was past, as Thor raised his arms to defend against the troll's punches. Their battle was hard-fought, no quarter asked nor given. First Thor struck the troll in its belly, but then the troll struck a blow on Thor's chest. Thor kicked his foe in the leg and heard the crack of bone, but even with a leg hobbled, the troll was able to backhand Thor so hard that he skidded across the square, coming to rest near where Sif fought her own troll.

"Need you aid, Thor?"

"Nay, fair Sif, tarry with your foe a while longer. I will show this knave that Thor is not one to be trifled with." Even as he spoke, Thor got to his feet and spied his hammer. Though still it would not return to him, he could clasp its haft in his hand.

But even as he lifted it, he knew something was amiss. Mjolnir was a tool of great power, and every time he held the hammer, Thor could feel its power almost as if it were a living thing.

What he held now was but dead weight.

So distressed was he over the seeming loss of his hammer that he failed to acknowledge the troll's speedy approach until it was almost too late. At the last second, Thor was able to roll with the troll's mighty punch, tumbling once again to the paving stones of the square. Had he not done so, surely the blow would have severed his head from his neck.

Again the troll laughed, raising his arms in premature triumph. "Is this the mighty thunder god of whom so many speak in fearful tones? For lo these many seasons I have heard Geirrodur and Grundor, Kryllik and Ulik speak in frightful whispers, cautioning us of Thor, for he is the mightiest of the Aesir and he will defeat you as he has defeated trolls for many ages."

Turning to scream at the heavens, the troll continued his rant. "I laugh at those pitiful fools who cringe in terror at Thor's might! I am Baugi! And today I will forevermore be known as Thorsbane, for I will have defeated the son of Odin!"

And then Thor belted Baugi in the jaw, sending the troll flying across the square and landing atop the Warrior's Walk.

"My thanks, Baugi, for your breathless rant," Thor said as he ran across the square toward the Walk, "for it gave me the opportunity to become less breathless myself and rejoin the battle properly."

He grabbed Baugi by the strap of his loincloth and threw him back toward the Yggdrasil monument. Though not as sturdy as the world tree itself, the monument was resilient enough to withstand the impact of a tossed troll.

"Be wary of boastful words, Baugi," Thor continued as he leapt down from the Walk toward the monument where the troll struggled to rise, "for it is actions by which one is judged, whether god, mortal, giant, dwarf—or troll."

Having holstered the now-powerless hammer in his belt,

Thor wielded it again as he landed at the foot of the monument, and swung it downward at Baugi's head.

Though seemingly no longer carrying Odin's enchantment, the hammer was solid enough. Mindful of its name, Thor used it to smash the head of the vain Baugi, backed by the immortal strength of the thunderer.

Baugi slumped to the grass at the base of the monument. He drew breath still, but he did not move.

"Rise, mighty Baugi. Face the god of thunder and defeat him as you boasted!"

When the insensate Baugi declined the invitation, Thor turned to see how fared his friends.

Sif had finished off her foe, and Hogun had done likewise for one of his. While Hogun swung his mace toward his remaining enemy, Sif had drawn off one of Fandral's sparring partners for herself. Meanwhile, Volstagg continued to regale the two prisoners of his expansive posterior with tales of bravery from his own youth.

Holding up his arms, Thor cried, "Minions of Baugi, behold your leader! He is defeated at the hands of the protector of Asgard! Yield now and you will be spared, or fight on and join foul Baugi in defeat!"

The trolls took very little time to mull. Hogun's foe held up his arms, and the two who faced Sif and Fandral did so but a moment later. As for Volstagg's audience, one of them cried, "Please, thunder god, either kill us or send us home to the Realm Below, but spare us further crushing by this crushing bore!"

"Hmph!" Volstagg said as he slowly and awkwardly rose to his feet. "So very like a troll to fail to appreciate the wisdom of their betters. Why I recall one time—"

Fandral held up a hand and said, "Enough, voluminous one! Thor promised to *spare* them if they yielded."

Volstagg let out a *harrumph* of annoyance, but spoke not further. Thor couldn't help but chuckle as he retrieved his helmet from the ground and replaced it on his head.

Thor then regarded each of the surviving trolls in succession. "Fandral, Hogun, and Volstagg shall escort you and your dead back to the Realm Below. Be sure to tell your fellows of Baugi's ignominious defeat, and that Asgard still stands."

The trolls said nothing, simply collecting their dead and then moving toward the outskirts of the city alongside the Warriors Three. Thor noted that the two on whom Volstagg had sat were walking gingerly.

Turning to his oldest friend as well as the woman who meant second-most to him among all the females of the gods of Asgard (behind only Frigga), Thor said, "Balder, Sif, I would beg that you bring Baugi to the dungeons that the troll may await my father's justice."

Sif said, "Of course."

"What of you, Thor?" Balder asked.

"I must go to the All-Father directly." He held up the hammer. "Something has happened to Mjolnir. Still do I sense its presence, yet what I hold here in my hand is but an ordinary tool. I doubt the trolls are responsible—if Baugi had such magicks as could neutralize my hammer, they would not have been so easily defeated this day."

A voice came from all around them in the square. "Ah, but where's the fun in an *easy* defeat, brother?"

Loki Laufeyson materialized in front of Thor. No doubt he had used his sorcerous abilities to shield himself from the battle until it was over. Ever the coward's route did Loki travel.

Odin's adopted son grinned widely and held out his arms, garbed in the green robes he preferred. "You did well, Thor, to defeat Baugi and his minions without your oh-so-precious hammer."

Reaching out with his empty hand, Thor clasped Loki's robes and pulled the trickster close. "Speak, Loki, what have you done to Mjolnir?"

His voice remaining calm despite the threat of violence from his brother—not to mention Balder and Sif, who had unsheathed their swords at Loki's appearance—the son of Laufey said, "I have done nothing to your hammer. I have, however, altered the air around it. If you don't mind. . . ?" To accentuate the point, Loki looked down at Thor's left hand.

Frowning, Thor let go of his adopted brother's raiment, and only then did Loki make a simple gesture.

Even as the false hammer crumbled to dust in Thor's right hand, the very air near the stairs to the Temple of Titans seemed to shimmer, revealing Mjolnir itself on the ground where Thor had earlier dropped it.

Clapping his hands to get rid of the remaining dust of the false hammer, Thor then held his own right hand out and Mjolnir flew to it, as ever.

Wrapping his fingers around the haft, Thor said, "What possible reason could you have for such a ploy, brother?"

"I did observe Baugi and his dozen thugs as they approached the halls of Asgard."

"Then why," Sif asked, "did you not aid us in defending the city against them?"

"I have always felt, fair Sif, that the defense of Asgard against such base foes is best left to those of greater physical strength and concomitant limitation of intellect. However, I did observe, in case Baugi's campaign threatened my own interests, and what I saw was a simple battle against a dull-witted fool." Again Loki grinned. "So I took the fool's hammer away."

Thor shook his head. "Were there two of you, Loki, you would comprise a single wit."

"And for how many decades have you been working on *that* bit of jocularity, thunder god? Nonetheless, my jest is complete, and so now I return to—"

"I say nay, Loki, you will come with me to see the All-Father." As Thor spoke, he placed the hammer in its strap upon his belt. The familiar weight was a tremendous comfort.

"For what purpose?" Now the trickster sounded nervous. "I did reveal myself precisely to avoid a confrontation with our father."

"You say you observed the trolls' approach, but even Heimdall himself did not spy Baugi and his legion until they were within the city gates. You will explain to Odin how you were able to discern what the guardian of the rainbow bridge could not."

Shaking his head, Loki started to make gestures to form the spell that would take him away to his keep. "I will do no such thing. The time of Loki is not to be wasted on such frivolities."

Again Thor reached out, grabbing Loki's arm before it could complete the sigil. "You will come at my urging—or at Odin's. Choose."

Loki did pretend to consider his options, but in truth he had no choice. Odin would, of course, do as Thor requested and summon Loki to speak before the All-Father. It was best if he not incur his adoptive father's wrath unnecessarily.

"Very well, brother, I will accompany you to Odin's throne room."

Leaving Balder and Sif to take care of Baugi, Thor and Loki proceeded to the palace, located at the very center of Asgard. Up the gleaming golden staircase they went, through the huge double doors guarded by two warriors—who, naturally, did not hesitate to allow ingress to the sons of Odin—and thence to the grand throne room.

They entered on the far side of the great space, which was large enough to hold hundreds of Asgardians, but which today was completely empty. Thor's footfalls echoed as they strode across the hall; Loki's own tread was light and silent.

Odin himself sat in the massive golden throne, his hands gripping the armrests, as his ravens, Hugin and Munin, flitted about his shoulders. The All-Father was receiving some manner of intelligence from the ravens, who served as Odin's eyes and ears throughout the Nine Worlds.

But as Thor and Loki approached the grand throne, Odin turned away from the ravens and fixed his one good eye on the pair of them. At the base of the stairs that led to the throne, both Thor and Loki removed their headgear and knelt before the ruler of Asgard. Thor did so quickly and eagerly, Loki slowly and reluctantly.

"Welcome, my sons. I assume you bring glad tidings of the troll invasion of our fair city?"

"Indeed, Father." Thor rose, as did Loki next to him. "With the aid of Balder, Sif, and the Warriors Three, the trolls were driven from Asgard's streets. Fandral, Hogun, and Volstagg are returning all to the Realm Below, save their leader Baugi, whom Balder and Sif are even now escorting to the dungeons, to await your judgment, All-Father."

"And judge him I shall, at a later time. But now I wonder why Loki's name is left out of the list of those who drove the trolls from our home."

Loki provided his most insincere grin. "I held myself in reserve, All-Father. A half-dozen gods seemed more than sufficient to deal with an arrogant, ambitious upstart such as Baugi."

Thor whirled to face his brother. "How now, brother? Why do you characterize Baugi thus?"

Loki blinked. "I beg your pardon?"

"Upstart, yes, Baugi was, but to name him as arrogant and ambitious indicates a knowledge of his character beyond what could be observed in battle."

"To you, perhaps," Loki said dismissively. "Some of us are keener observers of character than others."

Looking back at Odin, Thor added, "In addition, Loki did claim to observe Baugi's approach before Heimdall—and he hindered me in battle by keeping Mjolnir from my hand."

Up until this moment, Odin had been the picture of calm. He knew that matters were well in hand, for were they not, his sons' entry into the throne room would have been urgent and quick rather than calm and slow.

However, once Thor mentioned yet another example of treachery from Loki, Odin's face grew hard and he stared at his adopted son with his one good eye.

"Does Thor speak true, Loki?"

"Technically, yes, I—temporarily!—cloaked his hammer in a shroud of invisibility and covered it in an eldritch casing that physically restrained it from returning to Thor's hand. However, I did leave him a simulacrum of Mjolnir that served its purpose rather well. Indeed, his final defeat of Baugi was done with the ersatz hammer I provided him."

Fists clenched, Thor started to move menacingly toward his adopted brother. "All you 'provided,' dear brother, was a means by which Baugi could defeat me."

Loki did back up a step, but his expression remained one of amusement. "Ah, so the rumors are true, then? Without his hammer, Thor is as helpless as an old woman? Without the crutch of Mjolnir, he is truly crippled?"

"Enough!" Odin cried out, his voice echoing across the empty hall, cutting off any attempt by the thunder god to reply to the slander. "Your japes and jests are ill-timed, Loki, and foolish."

"Did the All-Father not receive notification that his second son is the god of mischief?"

"He did," Odin said slowly, "and I would ask in return if the god of mischief recalls that Odin is the All-Father, all-seeing and all-knowing. Whatever I do not see myself with my good eye is observed by Heimdall from his post or by my faithful ravens." Odin gestured behind him and to the right at the secondary throne, where Hugin and Munin had alighted. At times when Odin was unable to rule Asgard for whatever reason—lost in battle, say, or having succumbed to the Odinsleep—his proxy ruler would do so from that smaller throne, as none were willing to occupy the All-Father's seat. "Indeed, Hugin and Munin just informed me that they espied Loki Laufeyson travelling to the Realm Below himself not so long past. I wonder now if your observation of Baugi's personality traits came, not from seeing him in battle this day, but from a prior meeting? One in which you provided the troll with the means to enter Asgard's gates unnoticed by Heimdall or any other sentry?"

Loki said nothing in reply at first, finally speaking in a much less amused voice. "The All-Father's accusation is—"

"Completely in character for Loki," Thor interrupted, and his tone was, in turn, far more amused than it had been.

Odin rose and pointed an accusatory finger at his adopted son. "Loki, you have endangered the Realm Eternal, both by conspiring with Baugi and his minions and by interfering with Thor's ability to drive him back."

"Oh, *please.*" Now Loki rolled his eyes. "The only thing Baugi endangered in the Realm Eternal was a few of the paving stones in the square outside the Temple of Titans. Surely Asgard's protectors are well able to handle thirteen trolls without straining themselves. I daresay even Volstagg could have defeated them by his lonesome." He snorted. "By boring them to death, no doubt. Still, no lasting harm was done."

Unimpressed by Loki's excuses, Odin asked, "And does Loki now number precognition among his talents? True, there are none braver than the six who faced the trolls, but *every* warrior has his end some day, and sometimes that end is ignominious indeed. Today might well have been that day, and it would have been Loki who was responsible. Therefore, it is my judgment—"

"Judgment?" Loki drew himself to his full height in outrage. "I did nothing that warrants—"

"Be *silent!*" For only the second time, Odin raised his voice, but this time the very walls did rattle from his bellow.

Wisely, Loki remained quiet.

"It is my judgment that you be confined to your keep for a period of one month. Hugin, Munin, *and* Heimdall will all observe your home with their keen eyes. Should you at any point remove yourself from your quarters, you will find the All-Father's punishment to be far more severe."

"Father, I—"

But Odin wished not to hear Loki's craven plea. "I have spoken! Begone from my presence! Thor, escort your brother to his punishment."

Thor once again knelt before his liege. "With pleasure, Father."

Grabbing Loki's left arm, Thor led the trickster forcibly from the hall. Loki kept looking back at the throne, which Odin had retaken, but Odin's visage remained hard and unyielding.

The two ravens flitted about the heads of both gods as they departed, making it clear that Loki would not have an unobserved moment for the next several weeks, and that his sentence commenced immediately.

As they left the hall, Loki shook his head, a miserable expression on his countenance. "Absurd. Simply absurd. I play a simple prank, and *this* is the All-Father's punishment?"

"I would say, *dear* brother," Thor said with a smile as wide as that used by Loki prior to Odin's judgment, "that you got off easy. Asgard itself was invaded by an enemy. For the All-Father to punish you merely by grounding you, as they say on Midgard, he is being far kinder than perhaps you deserve."

Loki fixed Thor with a withering look. "You'll forgive me, *dear* brother, if I put little stock in what *you* feel I deserve."

"What I feel matters little, for it is what the All-Father feels, and what he decrees, that all Asgardians must heed."

"So I am regularly reminded." Loki sighed heavily. "Ah, well. The joy of immortality is patience, and a month is but a blink of an eye. I shall occupy myself with some tasks about the keep, and the month will pass ere long. And rest assured, Thor, that my hands shall *not* be idle come the end of my sentence."

"And *you* may rest assured, Loki, that Thor will be ready for whatever foolish plan you might concoct."

"Speaking of himself in the third person the entire time, no doubt," Loki muttered as they proceeded to his keep, and the commencement of his exile.

He was sure that his house arrest would go by quickly.

# CHAPTER TWO

L oki's house arrest did not go by quickly.

By the middle of the second day, he felt as if he'd been trapped within the walls of his keep for centuries.

It was all well and good to say to Thor that he had "tasks" about the keep, but in truth all that needed doing was drudge work. He had sprites and other magickal creatures to perform such menial duties for him. Indeed, they were under strict orders to perform them when he was away from the keep. Not only would the second son of Odin never lower himself to restock the pantry or dust the furniture or clean the privy or organize his scrolls, he refused to even be present when the magickal creatures indentured to him engaged in those tasks.

"So this is what it's come to, Father?" Loki cried out to the heavens. He doubted that Odin was listening, though no doubt his ridiculous birds were and would relay his ranting. "Have none of the Aesir even a spot of a sense of humor anymore? The trolls were nothing, a mere diversion for the gods of Asgard. I did Thor and the others a *favor* by giving them a foe to fight. My brother is never happier than when he's clumping creatures on the head, and I gave him the opportunity! And, yes, I hid Mjolnir, but let's face it, Thor has become far too reliant on that silly hammer. What if someday he loses it? Or breaks it? Or someone else becomes 'worthy' and takes it from him, as has already happened more than once? I was *helping* my brother—and yes, playing a bit of a joke, but shouldn't siblings have japes and jests between them?"

"Talking to yourself, my son?"

Whirling around, Loki saw that Frigga stood in his sitting room, a warm smile on her face.

"Yes, Mother, I am. It's my only guarantee of intelligent conversation."

After a moment, he sensed that it was in actuality an astral projection of his adoptive mother. Frigga only very occasionally employed the magickal gifts of her Vanir heritage, but Loki knew that she had plenty of sorcerous talents in her own right. Indeed, it was she who originally encouraged him, as a youth, to pursue such arts when he proved less interested in the art of combat than his adoptive brother.

"My apologies for the state of the keep, Mother, but I wasn't expecting guests. Odin's house arrest carried with it the implication that I am to bear it alone."

"His sentence only applied to you, my son. Any may come see you."

"Wonderful. I suppose I can expect Thor to come by and gloat at his earliest convenience."

"Unlikely—and I would not permit it if he wished to."

Loki blew out a breath. "Thank you, Mother. I don't suppose you could appeal to Father's better nature? Ask him for a less onerous sentence than being stuck batting about my home?"

"I'm afraid not, my son." Frigga's smile became more wry. "When Odin told me of his punishment, I told him that, if anything, he went too easy on you."

Drawing himself upright, Loki stared incredulously at her. "I *beg* your pardon?"

"Loki, you took Thor's hammer from him in the middle of battle against a troll. He could've been killed."

Snorting, Loki said, "I do not have that kind of luck. The fates would never favor me with so easy a death for him."

"He is your brother, Loki—and he is my son."

"And he has faced far worse than an out-of-his-depth troll with delusions of grandeur, and survived. I knew well that he would survive this." He chuckled. "Oh, Mother, the look on his face when he held out his hand and Mjolnir did not fly to his grasp—for that alone, the entire jest was worth it!"

"If it were truly worth it, my son, then you should bear your punishment without complaint."

Loki opened his mouth and then closed it, as he had no response to that. Damn his mother and her infernal logic . . .

Frigga moved closer to Loki. Instinctively, he reached out to her, but she, of course, had no substance.

"I do not understand why you must constantly play this game with your brother. The constant torment . . ."

"I am the god of mischief, Mother. Tormenting my fellows is my very purpose. I could no more cease to 'play this game,' as you put it, than Thor could stop producing thunder and lightning, or Heimdall could stop seeing over great distances, or Volstagg could stop eating."

Giving a mock-shudder, Frigga said, "Truly a black day in the Nine Worlds it would be if Volstagg were to stop eating. Why, our stores might actually overflow!"

Joining in the mocking, Loki added, "The chefs of Asgard might be permitted to sleep, as they will no longer need to work through the night and day to provide enough victuals for the endless stomach of the Lion of Asgard."

Both mother and son shared a laugh at that, and Loki found himself calm for the first time since Thor hauled him off to see Odin.

"Thank you, Mother."

"For what?"

"For caring."

"Oh, my dear, dear son." Frigga reached out as if to cup Loki's cheek in her hand, but stopped short, remembering that her presence was eldritch and not physical. "I have always cared. I have always loved you. Indeed, it is because I love you so much that I am so constantly disappointed when you engage in such petty and dangerous frivolity as this."

Loki had flinched at her insubstantial gesture, and then shook his head and moved away, the jocular moment now gone. His voice harder and more distant, he said, "There are those who would say that Loki is not capable of returning the love you espouse for him."

Frigga, however, refused to follow Loki into his suddenly more somber mood, the wry smile returning instead. "There are those who say that Loki's tendency to speak of himself in the third person shows an excess of pretension. Regardless, I have never cared for the gossip of others. I know both my sons, and know full well how they feel—regardless of whether or not they may express those feelings."

Turning to face his mother once more, Loki said, "Regardless, Mother, even as you express your disappointment, it is leavened with the expression of your love. That has not gone unnoticed." Again turning away, he added, "From the All-Father, all I perceive is the disappointment."

"His disappointment is only so great because his love is equally great. I know it is hard to see. Odin rules all of Asgard, and the weight of that responsibility is heavy indeed. But it makes it difficult to show his true feelings."

Loki turned and gave his mother a half-smile. "Somehow I suspect that the thunder god never doubts the affection Father has for him."

"Odin sentenced Thor to live life as a crippled mortal with no knowledge of his heritage. I believe that Thor may have wavered in his belief of Odin's love for him when the deception was revealed."

Shaking his head, Loki regarded Frigga with wonder. "You do have quite the gift, Mother."

"Thank you, my son." Frigga's image started to fade a bit. "I must leave you now, and tend to the throne room."

Loki frowned. That was Odin's domain solely. "Why the throne room?"

"Only to keep an eye on things. Asgard is quiet since the trolls were driven away, and Odin has grown restless and decided to go on one of his—excursions."

At that, Loki rolled his eyes. "Let me guess—he has disguised himself as an old man with one eye? It amazes me that he ever fools anyone when he goes on those—excursions, as you call them."

Frigga shrugged. "He enjoys pretending to be someone else. It is enough for him to remove his royal armor and his eyepatch and put on a battered old cloak. His disguises need not be as clever physically as your illusions, my son. Just by being an ordinary old man on horseback, people do not believe he is the All-Father. After all, would the ruler of Asgard travel alone on the road to Jotunheim?"

"That depends upon the horse. Is he riding Sleipnir?"

"Of course." Frigga chuckled. "The horse *looks* like an ordinary mount to the casual observer."

"Well, there you go—I have never *casually* observed anything. It is how I have thrived all these centuries."

"In any event, my son, I must go." Frigga gave Loki one last, loving look. "Be well, Loki."

Even as the astral image faded, Loki said, "That will be very difficult while I'm trapped in this house!"

Though he was glad of his mother's company for the brief time she was present, it served only to exacerbate his loneliness now that she was gone. With a sigh, he retired to the pantry. The talk of Volstagg's appetite had made him hungry, and his latest delivery of the golden apples of immortality had arrived that morning.

Idunn, the goddess in charge of the apples, took her duties seriously, including delivering a supply of the apples in her care to each of the Aesir every month. Every god of Asgard, regardless of his or her status within the realm, was given the same delivery. Idunn's neutrality was as strong as that of the fates, and even Loki did not dare challenge it, for that was the one way to risk being removed from her delivery list. He could anger Thor, Odin, Balder, Frigga, Sif, the Warriors Three, Heimdall, or anyone else in the Nine Worlds, and Idunn would care not. But if he dared anger her?

Of course, it might have been enjoyable for the trickster to do something to affect *all* of the apples. Loki's musing on this possible plan of action was cut short upon his entry into the pantry by a simply horrible smell. He'd not encountered a stench this awful since his visit to the Realm Below to convince Baugi to invade Asgard.

But trolls had yet to be introduced to the concept of bathing, while Loki prided himself on his fastidiousness.

So he was appalled to see that the pantry had gone to seed. Leftover foodstuffs from the first day of his house arrest had not yet been disposed of, dishes and cutlery had not yet been cleaned and put away, and flies buzzed about, one flying right in Loki's face.

Swatting away the insect, Loki immediately summoned the sprites who were tasked with the keeping of his keep.

Three tiny, winged, green-skinned creatures appeared before him, flitting about the pantry alongside the flies.

"Speak, speak, Loki Laufeyson!"

"Tell us how we may service the trickster god!"

"The god of mischief commands us!"

"Yes," Loki said impatiently, "I do. And have. Your job is to keep my home neat and clean, yet *look* at this place!"

The sprites flew around the pantry, noses wrinkled, and then all alighted before him side by side.

"We do as we are bid!"

"Clean the pantry we shall!"

"As soon as next you depart!"

Loki winced. He rarely was in his keep for more than a few days at a time, as there was always some new scheme to conceive, some campaign of mischief to enact. Therefore, the sprites had been under strict instruction to do their domestic chores only when Loki himself did not have to witness it. Under normal circumstances, Loki's comings and goings provided ample opportunity for the sprites to heed his directive.

But Odin's house arrest had changed things, and he needed to adjust his commands to the sprites accordingly.

Striding to the burlap sack containing this month's supply of apples, Loki said, "I have been forced to remain in the keep for the time being, so for now, you may perform your duties regardless of whether or not I am present."

The sprites all exchanged nervous glances with each other.

"If that is what the trickster desires . . ."

"If truly Loki is sure . . ."

"We will, of course, do as the second son of Odin demands . . ."

Loki shook his head as he pulled one of the golden apples from the sack. "Yes. Yes, you will. And do it quickly!" He took a huge bite out of the apple to emphasize his point, swatted another fly that flew in front of his face, and left the pantry in a huff.

At this point, Loki was fed up with everything. With Odin and his arbitrary punishments meted out against his son, who simply did what he was supposed to do as god of mischief. With Thor and his dull wits and insistence on dragging Loki to Odin in the first place. With Baugi and his minions, who couldn't even put up a decent fight against Thor and his idiot friends, even though Thor himself was relieved of his greatest weapon. With those friends, who insisted on joining Thor; had Balder, Sif, and the Warriors Three minded their own business, the trolls would have trounced Thor royally. With the sprites and their tiresome literal-mindedness, leading to a most filthy pantry. Even with his mother, who could have come in person and could have stayed longer.

Entering his bedroom, Loki fell more than sat on his bed and took a few more bites of his apple.

Once he consumed all but the core of the apple, he tossed it aside, hoping as he did so that the sprites would know to clean it up even though he remained. They might well have only followed his instruction with regard to the pantry and let the rest of the keep go to pot.

And then another fly came in and settled on his nose.

He swatted the fly, and then sighed, wondering if he should go back to the pantry and instruct the sprites to specifically get rid of the flies.

Then he wondered if he could cast a spell that would send all the flies to wherever Odin was disguised and riding Sleipnir.

And then, suddenly, it came to him.

Throwing his head back, Loki laughed long and hard.

It was perfect. Even Heimdall would be fooled.

First, Loki changed into his bedclothes. True, it was midday, but he would always be able to defend the notion of an afternoon nap as resulting from the boredom of house arrest.

Then he began composing a somewhat complicated spell that would create a simulacrum of himself. He also prepared to change his own shape, something Loki could do as naturally as breathe, though the transformation he planned would be of particular difficulty.

In order for his newly conceived plan to work, he would have to do three things at once, and two of those things could not be accomplished until the third was done, and that was out of Loki's control.

And then the third thing finally did happen, as he knew it would: another fly buzzed about his face.

At once, Loki performed the three actions required to enact his cunning plan.

He clapped his hands together to crush the fly between his palms.

He changed his own shape from his familiar dark-haired form to that of a fly.

He activated the simulacrum.

The eldritch doppelgänger occupied the exact space that Loki vacated when he made himself into a creature the size and shape of an insect, down to the clapped hands. Loki was confident that even Heimdall's keen vision would not be able to detect the switch.

Even as the fly he swatted fell to the floor, dead, Loki himself flew toward the keep's window in the form of that insect. He also instructed the simulacrum to yawn, lie down on the bed, and sleep.

Smiling to himself while shaped as a fly, Loki knew that Heimdall and Odin's ravens would see only that Loki had tried to kill a fly and then given up and gone to sleep.

And now he was once again free to move about the Nine Worlds as he pleased!

But as soon as he fled his keep, he realized that he wasn't sure where to go. So thoroughly had he accepted Odin's decree that he had given no thought to what he might do if freed, since that day had seemed so far away until his insect-related brainstorm.

As he flew upward, he caught a glimpse of Hugin and Munin, and upon seeing Odin's pet birds, he knew what he had to do.

Frigga had said that the All-Father was taking his horse on the road to Jotunheim. So Loki flew in that direction to see what Odin was up to and how he might interpolate himself into his adoptive father's adventure.

# CHAPTER THREE

No one knew where Hrungnir got his golden horse.

The fearsome frost giant had obtained a large, gold-maned mount, whom he had named Goldfaxi. And since acquiring the horse, no one had been able to defeat Hrungnir.

Some say he won the steed in a game of chance with the dwarves. Others said it was a game of skill, but that seemed unlikely. Dwarves are too canny to be defeated by a giant by anything other than luck or strength, and no dwarf would enter a contest of strength with a giant, especially not one of Hrungnir's might.

Others say he stole the horse from the stables belonging to Karnilla, Queen of the Norns. At one time, such a notion would have been unthinkable, but Karnilla was kidnapped once by another giant, Utgard-Loki, and since then, the Norn Queen's reputation had suffered. Nonetheless, many of the giants who followed Hrungnir feared retribution from Karnilla.

Another story was told that Hrungnir purchased the mount from a stable on Midgard, where the mortals had used their science to breed a horse of great speed and power.

Regardless of where Hrungnir obtained the mount, Goldfaxi had proven to be a great boon. The horse was large enough to support the giant's girth, yet still fleet enough of hoof to outrun any mount in the Nine Worlds.

Or so Hrungnir claimed. In any event, the results spoke for themselves. Hrungnir and the other giants who had pledged loyalty to him had not yet lost a campaign since Goldfaxi became his steed.

On this day, Hrungnir led his followers to the outskirts of Nornheim. When he announced his plan, his trusted lieutenant, Thjasse, spoke to him in private.

"Is this wise, mighty Hrungnir? Karnilla is a vengeful queen, and if you approach her with the very horse that you stole from her—"

But Hrungnir only laughed boisterously. "Do not believe all the stories you hear, clever Thjasse. I have no reason to fear anything from the Norn Queen—though perhaps after today, I shall give her reason to fear me, eh?" Again, Hrungnir laughed, and he spurred Goldfaxi onward.

While Thjasse and the other giants struggled to keep up with their leader's golden-maned steed, Hrungnir rode ahead until he reached a farm located on the outskirts of Karnilla's lands.

A group of men and women who were tilling the fields saw Hrungnir, and put down their hoes and shovels and wheelbarrows and faced the giant.

One of the women stepped forward as Hrungnir brought Goldfaxi to a whinnying halt. "We know who you are."

"I should hope you are aware of Hrungnir the Mighty,

Hrungnir the Brawler, Hrungnir the conqueror of all he meets and conquers!"

The farmers exchanged a glance, and even Hrungnir realized that his phrasing was poor. But he was no Asgardian god with their flowery speech. He was a man of action.

"And what I meet today," he added quickly, "is you. My followers are hungry, and we will take some of your food."

"Without this food, we will starve," the woman said.

Hrungnir looked out at the fields, which were lengthy and full of plants in full bloom. "You are growing more food, far more than you shall need to feed yourselves."

"And what of winter?" the woman asked. "We must grow more than we need so we do not starve during the cold months, and so that we may be prepared in case of a bad harvest."

Hrungnir snorted. "Your future plans are of no interest to me, little farmers. I am Hrungnir, and I take what is mine."

"What if you are challenged?" the woman asked before Hrungnir could goad Goldfaxi onward.

Barking a cruel laugh, Hrungnir asked, "Who among you would challenge me?"

"Not you," the woman said. "Your horse. The reason *why* we know who you are is because of your steed. They say that Goldfaxi is faster than any horse in the Nine Worlds save Sleipnir, the steed of the All-Father himself."

"I would wager that even Odin's horse would be poorly matched against mine. So how would such as *you* challenge me?"

"Our horses are not fast, but they are strong. Goldfaxi may be fast, but can he pull a plow as well as our Alsvinnur?"

She pointed to the farm's large, brown horse, currently at rest but still tethered to the plow.

Again, Hrungnir laughed. "And what is your challenge, fair farmer?"

The woman bowed her head. "Alsvinnur was about to plow the north end of the field. Tomorrow, after he is rested, he is to plow the south end. Our challenge is thus: Alsvinnur will indeed plow the north end, and Goldfaxi the south. The two sections are of equal size. Should Alsvinnur finish first, you and your giants will leave us in peace."

Before the woman could continue, Hrungnir spoke. "And *when* Goldfaxi wins, you will not stand in our way as we take however much of your food we wish?"

"As you say. Do I have your word that you will keep to the bargain?"

Hrungnir's face grew serious. "On my word, fair farmer, Hrungnir the Mighty will abide by the terms of our wager."

"And I, Sveina, daughter of Herdis, subject of the Norn Queen, do also swear by Karnilla's crown that I too shall abide by the terms."

With that, Hrungnir dismounted Goldfaxi. By the time Thjasse and the others had caught up, some of the farmers had retrieved their spare plow and were in the process of hooking Goldfaxi up to it. Meanwhile, three others led Alsvinnur and his plow to the north end of the field.

Thjasse approached Hrungnir and asked, "What is happening, mighty Hrungnir? Why is Goldfaxi being tethered to a plow? That is the fate of old horses that no longer can be ridden. Surely that is not your valiant steed's destiny?"

"Not at all, Thjasse. The farmers have proposed a wager and I have accepted. Should Goldfaxi plow his half of the field faster than the plowhorse, we shall take what we wish without resistance."

Frowning, Thjasse said, "I assume you have found a way to guarantee victory?"

"Don't speak nonsense, Thjasse. 'Tis a wager, and a fine one at that. Besides, I have faith in my steed. Goldfaxi shall win, and then instead of being forced to kill and maim these farmers, they will tell tales to their fellows of Hrungnir's might without those tales being leavened by weeping for their dead and cries in pain from wounds."

"But what if Goldfaxi does not win?"

Hrungnir shrugged his mighty shoulders. "If Goldfaxi is *not* the strongest mount in the Nine Worlds, better to know it than not, wouldn't you say?"

Thjasse said nothing in response, thinking only that it was better to guarantee a tangible victory than hope for a moral one.

Sveina stood at the center of the field, holding up a handkerchief. "When I drop this cloth, the horses may start. Whoever reaches me first will win the wager."

Standing near Goldfaxi, Hrungnir waited for the cloth to

fall, while another farmer did likewise across the field, ready to goad Alsvinnur onward.

Amused by the whole thing, Hrungnir actually waited several seconds after Sveina dropped her kerchief before patting Goldfaxi on the rump. Even then, the gold-maned mount hesitated, unaccustomed to having to drag such a great weight.

But the giant's steed was made of sterner stuff, and he finally began his work—a full ten seconds after Alsvinnur commenced his.

Sure enough, by the time Alsvinnur was halfway through the north end of the field, Goldfaxi was fast approaching Sveina's position.

And when Goldfaxi arrived at the center of the field, while Alsvinnur still had a quarter of his land to toil through, all the giants gave a throaty cheer.

"Go, my loyal subjects!" Hrungnir cried out. "Take what food you wish from these farmers—but *only* food! Do not harm any of them, nor damage their things! Anyone who does so will answer to Hrungnir the Mighty!"

Thjasse and the other giants proceeded to the storehouse to raid it for food, while Hrungnir himself turned to untether his horse.

As he did so, he cast a glance at Sveina, whose visage spoke of a woman whose heart had broken. "You should be pleased, fair Sveina. Your bravery in the face of Hrungnir the Brawler was most impressive. That is why I spared your life and your things."

"And am I to fall to my knees in gratitude?" Sveina asked bitterly. "Without those stores, we will surely die this winter, only instead of the quick, violent death expected from an attack by your kind, it will be slow and painful."

"Be wary, Sveina, for Hrungnir's mercy is not unlimited. You still live, and where there is life, there is a chance. But you also defied the frost giants, and that never comes without a price to pay."

Within minutes, the giants had filled their burlap sacks with fruits and vegetables and herbs. In truth, they did not take as much as Sveina feared, for the giants preferred the meat of a beast that roamed the ground to the berries and roots that grew under it.

But food was food, and the giants still took more than their fill.

Hrungnir mounted Goldfaxi once again and rode away from Nornheim, having accomplished much for one day. They headed back in the direction of Jotunheim, Hrungnir leading his men in a song. They sang off-key, and Hrungnir was making up the words as he went along, making it hard for the others to keep up, but they all tried their best.

By the time the midday sun started its slow journey toward sunset, Hrungnir spied a lone traveler on the road from Asgard.

He was elderly, looking like one of the Aesir: large, by human standards, but still puny to one such as Hrungnir. His clothes were shabby and his white beard thick. Indeed, between the beard and the large floppy hat he wore, Hrungnir could scarce make out any of his face beyond his nose. A fly buzzed about the stranger's head, and he swatted at it absently, though the insect managed to avoid the old man's hand.

However, he rode a mount that was as impressive as any Hrungnir had seen outside of Goldfaxi himself.

"Ho, stranger!" Hrungnir cried out. "That is a fine steed you ride!"

The stranger bowed his head modestly, and spoke in a quiet tone. "My thanks, good sir. You, too, ride a most excellent horse."

"I had thought you to be of the Aesir, but perhaps not," Hrungnir said with a chortle. "None of those vain gods would ever speak with such respect to a frost giant. Indeed, were you not so old and infirm, I would expect you to unsheathe a sword at the very sight of me and mine."

Bowing his head, the old man said, "I am called Bolverk, and I wish no trouble, good sir. I am but a simple traveler who wishes to ride through these empty roads in peace."

And now Hrungnir let out a throaty laugh. "Truly you are not of Asgard, for all those who dwell in that thrice-cursed city know that peace is not the watchword of the frost giants—and certainly not that of Hrungnir the Mighty! But tell me of your mount, stranger. Rarely have I seen one with coat so bright and legs so strong. His gait is effortless even with the weight of both you and your supplies upon him. Whence comes this fine horse?"

"It is merely a family beast, good sir."

"What name has he?"

"None, good sir, for it is not the custom of my family to name those who cannot reply with voice to one's call."

Hrungnir laughed. "True enough."

"May I be on my way?" Bolverk asked humbly.

"Not as yet, Bolverk, for I must know which of our steeds would be fastest, my gold-maned mount, or your own unnamed beast."

The man who called himself Bolverk hesitated, for despite Hrungnir's beliefs, he was indeed of the Aesir, indeed the ruler of them all. Odin had changed into shabby clothing, mounted Sleipnir, the fastest horse in all the Nine Worlds, and hoped to take a lengthy ride alone in the lands between the realms. After the distasteful business with Loki and Thor and the trolls, he had hoped to have some time with only his own thoughts for company.

Word had reached him of Hrungnir and his horse Goldfaxi, and how they had been terrorizing the lands near Jotunheim. He had intended to address the issue before long, but after he had had a relaxing journey away from the burdens of his throne.

However, he was here now, facing Hrungnir, who was obviously confident in Goldfaxi's superiority. Had Odin truly been a simple traveler on an ordinary horse, that confidence would have been warranted.

"I challenge you, old man, to a race," Hrungnir said. "For I must know if Goldfaxi is truly the fastest in the land, and only through a race may it be determined."

"Do you not have faith in your mount, good sir?"

"In my own, yes, but in yours I can have neither faith nor surety, for they have not been tested against each other."

"And if I refuse this challenge?" It took all of Odin's will-power to keep his voice in the same humble tone he'd adopted for the role of Bolverk, for he found this giant's effrontery to be insulting.

"Then all the giants gathered here will take your steed from you and leave you for dead on this road. But," he added quickly, "the word of Hrungnir is his bond! You may ask the farmers who till the fields outside Karnilla's realm if you wish. They proposed a wager, and Hrungnir the Mighty did abide by it—and took only what was his by the terms of the arrangement, no more, no less."

"And what would the terms of *this* wager be?" Odin asked with Bolverk's quiet aspect, while again swatting at the fly that had harried him for half the trip from Asgard.

"Should you win the race, old man, you may continue on your way, unmolested by the frost giants. If you think this a poor reward, think of the alternative."

"And should you win?"

Hrungnir smiled. "Then I will claim your horse as my own, for the Brawler must also have the second-fastest horse in the realm."

Odin considered the giant's offer. It was best to accept the wager, for that provided the best outcome. He knew Goldfaxi had no hope of riding faster than Sleipnir, and once the All-Father won the race, he would go on his way, with none the wiser regarding his disguise.

If he lost—well, Hrungnir would learn that "Bolverk" was no mere elderly traveler to be trifled with. Odin would not give up noble Sleipnir without a fight, and the All-Father could fight very well.

Hrungnir pointed to the nearby Algarrbyr Hill. "We will ride from here to the top of that hill, then turn and come back down again. My lieutenant, Thjasse, will stand here and await our return. Whoever reaches Thjasse first shall be the winner." Hrungnir then stared at the old man. "Swear by the River Gjoll that you will abide by the terms of our wager."

Beneath his thick white beard, Odin did smile. The giant was cleverer than the All-Father had given him credit for. That oath was one that no Asgardian would ever break. "I swear by the River Gjoll that I will turn my mount over to you, should you win our race."

Only a fool wagered with a giant, but even Odin dared not go back on an oath sworn on the river of the dead. Breaking that oath would result in that river claiming the oath-breaker in question. And so now he needed to have the faith in Sleipnir that he accused Hrungnir of not having in Goldfaxi.

Thjasse stood between the two horses as they faced Algarrbyr. "Be on your marks! Set, and—*go!*"

Hrungnir kicked Goldfaxi hard with his heel, prompting the horse to gallop. For his part, Odin leaned forward, loosening the reins to give Sleipnir freedom to move his head and simply squeezed lightly with both knees.

At first, the two horses were neck and neck. Odin did nothing to goad Sleipnir on, simply allowing him to gallop at his own pace. Meanwhile, Hrungnir repeatedly kicked his own mount, urging Goldfaxi to gallop ever faster.

When they reached the top of Algarrbyr, Sleipnir was able to easily turn around, guided with only the slightest tug of the reins and a low whisper.

Goldfaxi proved more recalcitrant, as Hrungnir had to wrestle with the steed to stop him from continuing down to the other side of Algarrbyr, and to instead turn around. By the time Goldfaxi was convinced to turn all the way around, Sleipnir had already started on the downward slope.

From that point on, the race was decided. Hrungnir continued to goad and kick Goldfaxi, but moving downhill served only to make Sleipnir faster, and the giant's mount simply could not keep the pace.

Odin passed Thjasse on the ground half a minute before Hrungnir arrived. It might as well have been an eternity for the giant.

For a brief instant, Odin was tempted to reveal his true self. That temptation was at least partly borne of the murderous expression on Hrungnir's face.

"How *dare* you make a mockery of me?!" Hrungnir cried.

Deciding to maintain the fiction of Bolverk at least long enough to see if the giant would abide by his word, Odin said quietly, "No, good sir, I did not. You challenged my horse and I to a race, and I won it. You made me swear by the River Gjoll that I would abide by the wager. Will you do the same? Or is the word of Hrungnir worth less than that of a simple old traveler?"

Hrungnir stared at the old man for many seconds. Thjasse and the other giants regarded their leader, wondering what he would do next.

Odin stared back at Hrungnir, mentally preparing a spell that would reveal his true nature to these impetuous giants.

But then Hrungnir's face softened. "Very well, Bolverk. I gave my word, and I will not have it known that Hrungnir the Mighty was an oath-breaker. Bad enough it is that I must now be known as having the *second* fastest steed in the Nine Worlds."

Once again, the fly that had menaced Odin flew in front of his face. Waving it away with his hand, he gently squeezed Sleipnir twice with his knees, and the steed began to slowly canter back toward Asgard. This, Odin had decided, was a close enough call, and it would be best if he returned to the city and his duties as its ruler. Including, it would seem, musing on ways to deal with Hrungnir's aggressiveness.

The fly, however, remained behind even as Odin moved on. The All-Father's proximity forced Loki to remain in his insectoid disguise, but he knew that Hrungnir would not listen to the counsel of a fly. But as he hoped, the All-Father's silly ruse provided Loki with an opening. Throughout the entire encounter, Loki had feared that the All-Father would reveal himself. But he did not, and that gave Loki precisely the opportunity he needed.

Once Sleipnir was out of sight, Loki whispered an incantation. His form shifted from that of a tiny fly to that of a giant serpent.

The giants cried out in shock at the sudden appearance of a serpent in their midst. Hrungnir simply stared at the new arrival. "What sorcery is this?"

"Fairly simple sorcery, all things considered," Loki said, his voice low and hissing thanks to the reptilian mouth that he now had to wrap around his words. "I am Loki, and I would have words with Hrungnir the Mighty."

"It has been some time since our paths crossed, trickster," Hrungnir said dryly, "but I recall you having two legs, black hair, and fair skin, none of which are in evidence before me now."

"As I said, fairly simple sorcery—but necessary, as I must keep my true form disguised lest Heimdall know I am in your midst." Loki saw no reason to discuss the specifics of his house arrest with such as these. "But rest assured, I am Loki. If I recall the genealogy of Jotunheim correctly, you are a nephew of Laufey, which makes us cousins."

Hrungnir laughed. "It seems my cousin has fallen on hard times if he must lower himself to speak before me as a mere serpent."

"Be that as it may," Loki said loudly to be heard over the chortling of Hrungnir and his fellow giants, "I am here to inform you that you have been tricked. The traveler who just defeated you and your precious gold-maned mount was none other than Odin himself."

Hrungnir drew himself up to his considerable full height. "You lie!"

"Often, yes, but not in this instance."

"Why would Odin have lowered himself to appear as so mean a presence?"

"For his amusement." Loki tried to chuckle, but it came out as a hiss. "It would not be the first time the All-Father has done this. He does love his disguises, and you did observe that 'Bolverk' had but one eye?"

Hrungnir looked away, waving a dismissive hand. "That means nothing."

"Who but great Sleipnir could so easily defeat your own Goldfaxi in a contest of speed?"

Hrungnir turned and gazed back over his shoulder at the serpentine form of the trickster.

Loki pressed his advantage. "Use your intellect, Hrungnir, or is your appellation of 'the Brawler' an indication that you know aught else? I suppose it is possible that there is another old man with a thick white beard and only one eye who possesses a horse that is faster than yours . . ."

As Loki had hoped, Hrungnir's response was a mighty cry to the heavens. "How *dare* he?! He did this deliberately to make me look a fool!"

Silently, Loki mused that he himself would take over that particular role, but aloud he only said, "Hardly surprising. Your steed has gained a reputation, and no doubt Odin wished to teach you a lesson in humility. He is fond of such games. Why, he once did the same to my hated brother, Thor."

Hrungnir turned to face the serpent directly. "What?"

"Thor was getting a bit full of himself—even more so than usual—and so Odin sent him to Midgard and entrapped him in the form of a crippled mortal. For the powerful thunder god to be trapped in so frail a form was a cruel and dire punishment indeed. And that was how Odin treated his own flesh and blood! Can you imagine he would treat you any better?"

Shaking his head, Hrungnir started to pace. "I should have known. And of course, old One-Eye came in disguise. Had Odin publicly challenged me, I would never have accepted it. Only a fool would wager against Sleipnir, and Hrungnir is no fool."

"Indeed not." Loki faked sincerity with those two words, as had the giant, for in truth Hrungnir had believed Goldfaxi to be the match even of Sleipnir before the race proved him wrong once and for all. "The question is, mighty Hrungnir, what shall you do about it?"

"All Asgard must pay for this indignity. For too long the Aesir have toyed with us, but it ends now. Tomorrow we attack Asgard and show Odin and his foolish gods that Hrungnir is *not* to be trifled with!"

"And it would be Loki's pleasure to assist you in this endeavor."

Thjasse spoke, then. "And what would the trickster demand in return for this assistance?"

"Indeed," Hrungnir said with a nod to his lieutenant. "Loki aids no one but himself."

"Can even the god of mischief not do a favor for family?" Another chuckle that translated into a hiss from his serpentine mouth. "Besides, just the knowledge that you will invade Asgard is enough to warm the cockles of my heart. I've no love for the Aesir, nor Asgard, nor Odin, nor his oh-so-favored son. In fact, should you kill Thor, I would be in your debt."

Gazing skeptically at the snake, Thjasse asked, "You would forego the pleasure of killing your hated brother yourself?"

In truth, Loki would have preferred to do the deed himself, as Thjasse said, but he doubted any of these giants truly had the wherewithal to eliminate his brother. However, he also spoke the truth when he replied: "Though I would prefer that the thunder god perish by my hand, I have come to the conclusion over the years that it is best to be rid of him regardless of the manner in which that is accomplished."

Hrungnir regarded Loki for several seconds before saying, "Very well. The invasion will commence at dawn!"

"And I will show you a pathway that is hidden even from Heimdall's sharp eyes." It was the same passage he had granted the trolls, one of many ways in and out of Asgard that Loki had either created or discovered over the centuries. The first had been a hole in the catacombs underneath the city, through which Loki had led the wolf gods and their allies. He'd found and made many since, and they had proven very handy at times. Sadly, none of them led directly to his keep, thus preventing him from using them to escape his current predicament.

"You will show Thjasse and me this pathway today, trickster," Hrungnir said, "and then tomorrow we will attack, and the day after, Asgard will fall!"

# CHAPTER FOUR

L oki's fatal flaw—well, in truth, he had several, but this was the one that mattered this day—was that he had a tendency to underestimate his rivals.

True, the passageways he'd provided for Baugi that enabled the trolls to penetrate the gates of Asgard were invisible to Heimdall—when Loki had so provided them. But Heimdall was not one to suffer a blind spot in his all-seeing expanse for long. From the moment the trolls arrived, he peered out amidst the gleaming spires of Asgard to locate the route the invaders took.

It was not long before he found it. And that discovery occurred before Loki's decision to assist Hrungnir in his intended attack on Asgard.

As a result, Hrungnir's invasion was not as much of a surprise as Loki had led the giant to believe.

From the outskirts of the city of Asgard—which he continued to flit about as a fly—Loki heard Heimdall's blaring of the Gjallarhorn, signaling that the city was under attack. Dawn had only just come, and Hrungnir couldn't have been within the city's gates yet. Based on the giant's plan, he would still be approaching the city from Loki's secret passageway beneath the Ida Plain.

Loki, however, did not concern himself. Just the fact that Asgard was invaded again gave him a warm and fuzzy feeling.

As for Heimdall, after sighting Hrungnir's invasion and blowing the Gjallarhorn, he was, as expected, visited by Hugin and Munin. After informing the ravens of what he saw, he remained steadfast at his post. Though he was, as ever, armed with Hofund, his enchanted sword, he did not join the battle, for his role as guardian of the Bifrost was too important. Indeed, it was at times such as this, when the city was in direct danger, that it became more imperative that Heimdall stand fast at the rainbow bridge, for it would not do for Asgard to be invaded from a second front even as they fought within the city walls.

Luckily, Heimdall's good sword arm was not necessary, for Asgard's defenders were well rested after their battle against Baugi and his trolls. Upon receiving Heimdall's message as relayed by his ravens, Odin immediately summoned Frigga, Thor, Sif, Balder, Fandral, Hogun, and not only Volstagg, but also Volstagg's wife Gudrun to his throne room.

Balder had been at his home, reading a letter from his former page, Agnar, who was visiting family in Vanaheim. Balder would have liked to have Agnar's good right arm by his side, but he would never arrive in time. Besides, the lad had earned the rest.


Sif, Fandral, and Hogun had been drinking in a tavern, wherein several foolish males had challenged Sif to arm wrestle. Not a single one was victorious over the "fair maiden," and each had to buy Sif a drink. Fandral had been encouraging people to bet, while Hogun kept his peace, as always. When the summons from Odin came, Sif defeated her last foe and instructed him to buy drinks for the house, since they were now being called away.

Volstagg had been home with Gudrun, putting their children to bed by telling them the story of how he singlehandedly drove Baugi and his trolls from the gates of Asgard. The children listened attentively and with bated breath, even though they knew full well that their father was but one of six who drove off the trolls. It didn't matter, though, because it was how their father told the story that delighted them.

As for Thor, he had been on his way to Midgard, for Thor was a protector with two mistresses. For all that the responsibility of protecting Asgard weighed upon him, protecting Midgard did the same. While the people of that world no longer worshipped him as a god—save for a few cultists, though Thor did not encourage such behavior—he still took his duties as the protector of mortals quite seriously.

For many centuries, he had vouchsafed the mortals against threats both terrestrial and otherwise, and never had he wavered in his loyalty to humans.

Still, Heimdall would not have blown the Gjallarhorn without reason. Just as Thor knew he could leave Asgard knowing that Sif and the others would protect the Realm Eternal, Thor also knew that Midgard would manage without him. That world was well-stocked with heroes—the mightiest of whom were Thor's comrades in the Avengers—and they would take up Thor's mantle of safeguarding the mortals until he could return.

Thor flew past Heimdall on the rainbow bridge, waving to the guardian as he headed back to the throne room. Alighting on the steps, he saw Volstagg and Gudrun approaching.

"Why have you brought your noble wife to this meeting, Volstagg? Not," he quickly added, "that her presence is anything but a benefit."

Gudrun inclined her head. "You flatter me, Thor, but all I may say for sure is that Odin's summons specified myself *and* my husband."

Volstagg indicated the door. "We shall never learn the truth of the matter if we stand out here."

"No indeed, my friend. Let us go to my father and learn what new foe threatens our home."

Upon arrival, they saw that Sif, Balder, and Volstagg's two boon companions were already present, as was Frigga.

"The Lion of Asgard has arrived, along with my lovely wife, and the noble Thor," Volstagg said.

Fandral grinned. "Aye, we knew of your arrival by the quaking of the ground."

Thor turned to the throne. "Speak, Father, and tell us why Heimdall has blown the Gjallarhorn and called us to battle."

Odin spoke plainly: "We are invaded by frost giants."

Fandral actually laughed. "Did we accidentally hang a sign on the city gates that reads, 'please invade'?"

Hogun, of course, did not laugh. "Regardless of the reason, the frost giants will not be allowed to succeed where the trolls failed."

Thor held his hammer aloft. "Hogun speaks true, Father. We shall again protect the city."

"Be off with you, then," Odin said. "As for my wife, you and Gudrun have an additional duty to perform."

Even as the men departed—Volstagg looking confusedly at Gudrun on his way out—Frigga said, "What would you request of us, husband?"

"The frost giants are dangerous, and I fear that my own arrogance is at least in part responsible for their current attack. I also would not put it past Hrungnir to try to get at the warriors of Asgard through our children. Therefore, Frigga, I must ask that you and Gudrun gather all the children of Asgard and bring them to safety within the Vale of Crystal."

"Will we be safe there?" Gudrun asked, skeptical that a crystal vale would serve as protection against giants.

Frigga put a reassuring hand on Gudrun's arm. "It is a place of magic, Gudrun, one that will protect any within its walls and keep out those who would invade it."

The wife of Volstagg nodded slowly. "Very well, Lady Frigga, if you say it is safe then I, of course, do not doubt you. But I must ask, All-Father, do you truly feel this to be necessary?"

"It has been some time since the frost giants came this close to Asgard. And Hrungnir has proven to be a deadly foe. I simply wish not to take the chance."

"Of course, my husband," Frigga said before Gudrun could object further.

Even as the two women departed Odin's presence in order to gather all the children of Asgard and bring them to safety, Thor did lead his dearest comrades to the Ida Plain to face off against another foe bent upon invading Asgard.

This time, though, they were able to engage Hrungnir and his subjects before they penetrated the heart of the city.

Astride Golfaxi, Hrungnir led the giants out of Loki's passageway and across the plain. He saw the half dozen warriors awaiting his arrival in the city and snarled. "Where is Odin? I would see him pay for making a fool of Hrungnir the Mighty!"

Whirling his hammer, Thor said, "Your foolishness is entirely of your own making if you believe that this day will end in aught but defeat for you and yours, Hrungnir."

Smiling, Hrungnir said, "If I must go through the thunder god to get to his father, then so be it! I will deposit your cooling corpse at Odin's feet like a dog at a funeral. And that funeral will be old One-Eye's!"

And then the time for words was past, as Hrungnir's giants stormed forward.

Thor tightened his grip on Mjolnir and instructed it to fly him toward the leader of the giants.

But Hrungnir expected such a frontal assault from the thunder god, and he raised his club and swung it like a player in the Midgard game of baseball. The impact sent Thor flying through the air into the heart of the Ida Plain.

The others attempted to take on Hrungnir in Thor's place, but all five were soon occupied by the mighty one's subjects.

Sif found the way to Hrungnir blocked by three giants.

"Ho," the largest one said, "'tis a maiden of Asgard!"

"She is comely for one so short," said the smallest one, who still stood head and shoulders taller than Sif.

The middle one chortled. "Perhaps she will massage our bodies to relax us when we have conquered this city."

"The only touch you will receive from me is that of my blade!" And with those words, Sif leapt at the largest, who was so confounded by the very notion of a woman warrior that he merely stood agape as Sif's blade met his throat.

Angered, the small one raised his axe. "You killed Kare!"

The medium one whirled his mace. "He was our brother! Let's get her, Pal!"

"You betcha, Gamni!"

Sif raised her own sword. "You will join your brother ere long."

Pal and Gamni both charged at Sif, a frontal attack she easily dodged by ducking under their high reach. She attempted to thrust her sword upward to strike one of the brothers in the gullet as she dodged, but she was unable to land the blow.

Rolling on her left shoulder, she got to her feet and readied herself for the next attack.

Gamni again whirled his mace and swung it toward Sif, and she again ducked under it. But then she thrust her sword arm upward and snagged the mace's chain, which wrapped around her armored limb. She then reached out with her other arm and yanked the chain farther up toward the spiked ball at its end, redirecting the ball toward Pal.

The ball crushed Pal's hideous face, and the small giant fell to the ground.

Gamni's face fell. "No! Pal! You killed him with my weapon!"

"You have a keen grasp of the obvious, Gamni," Sif said, extricating her arm from the chain. "Now yield, or join them with Hela in the realm of the dead!"

To Sif's complete lack of surprise, Gamni chose not to yield, instead lunging at her, arms outstretched.

He tackled her as she stood fast, sword outstretched, and they both fell to the ground in a heap. Gamni's massive form was like a dead weight atop Sif, and she feared he would crush her from that alone, never mind whatever further attack he might now commit to.

But that further attack did not come, and Sif soon realized that the dead weight atop her was well and truly dead. She assumed that Gamni had fallen on her sword.

Gathering up every inch, every muscle, Sif pushed as hard as she could, and managed to roll Gamni's body off her. Catching her breath, she looked over to see that the giant, now on his back, indeed had her blade protruding from his chest, as she had guessed.

Even as Sif fought the three giant brothers, the Warriors Three stood before Hrungnir himself, astride his gold-maned horse, surrounded by a phalanx of giants on foot who raised their weapons to prevent Fandral, Hogun, and Volstagg from such a frontal assault as Thor had attempted.

But the Warriors Three did not allow such trivial concerns as a dozen giants stand in the way of their desire to trounce Hrungnir.

His great longsword Fimbuldraugr upraised, Fandral led the charge, diving directly into the fray by leaping through the air. As he came down toward two of the giants, he slashed at them both before landing on the head of a third.

A grin forming underneath his thick blond mustache, Fandral cried out, "Hogun! A gift for you!" as he again leapt in the air, being sure to kick off the head of the giant he'd landed upon.

The force of his kick sent the giant sprawling toward the ground, but his progress was impeded by Hridgandr, the mace of Hogun. The grim one swung his great weapon into the giant's face, crushing the creature's outsized nose.

Fandral leapt to another giant's head and from that vantage point was able to smack another with the flat of his blade before again leaping and kicking to drive his temporary mount toward the ground.

"And one for you, voluminous one!" Fandral cried to Volstagg.

"Only one?" Volstagg asked as he reached back and then walloped the giant with a crushing right hook, which redirected the unfortunate giant to land atop the one whose face Hogun had pulverized. "You do insult the Lion of Asgard, Fandral, by only giving him *one* foe to vanquish!"

Hogun, typically, said nothing, instead sliding across the ground and using his mace to trip two of the giants, sending them both stumbling groundward.

However, they too found their journey to the dirt impeded by the fists of Volstagg. "See, Fandral? Hogun does appreciate Volstagg's prowess, for he gives me two giants to thrash!"

Normally, Fandral would reply to Volstagg's egotistical ramblings only by mocking them, but no appropriately cutting retort came to his lips. So he said nothing as he sheathed his sword and leapt to another giant, while Volstagg delivered a pair of uppercuts which sent both Hogun's giants flying to land atop the other two.

Fandral now hung onto the shoulders of one of the giants, dangling from the creature's back as if he were a cape. The giant struggled, trying to reach behind himself to grab the dashing one. For his part, Fandral took advantage of the giant's stumbling struggles to kick at his fellows. When the giant lumbered over to where the four giants lay atop each other, Fandral let go of the right shoulder. Reaching for his blade, he again unsheathed Fimbuldraugr from its scabbard and ran the giant through.

Even as the creature fell on top of his four insensate comrades, Fandral leapt to the head of another giant—but this one was ready for his assault and grabbed Fandral around the waist.

Fandral tried to gasp in pain, but even that was denied him as the giant's iron grip kept him from drawing breath.

Hogun had just tripped another giant for Volstagg to clout

when he saw that Fandral was snagged. Without hesitating, he twirled Hridgandr and threw the mace toward the giant's head.

Though the giant did not fall, the impact of the mace against his temple did cause him to loosen his grip on Fandral, enough so that he was able to push apart the giant's fingers enough so that he could leap away, landing on the ground right next to Volstagg.

"Ho, Fandral, have you decided to at last join in the fight instead of dancing about like a will-o'-the-wisp?"

Long accustomed to ignoring Volstagg's badinage for the good humor that it was, Fandral merely said, "I see no reason for you to have all the fun, voluminous one."

"Then let us thrash these unruly giants together!"

As the Warriors Three continued their battle against the giants protecting Hrungnir, Balder stood against a half dozen giants of his own.

"Be wary of Balder, my brothers," one of them said.

Another said, "He is alleged to be Asgard's greatest warrior, even greater than Thor!"

"Bah," said a third, "he's all talk and no action."

"Don't be so sure of that!" cried the fourth, who cringed a bit.

The fifth said, "'Twas he who singlehandedly gave Utgard-Loki his greatest defeat."

To Balder's surprise, the sixth said nothing, choosing instead to simply growl.

With a smile beneath his flat-horned helm, Balder said,

"'Twas not singlehanded, for I had aid from my friends in bringing Utgard-Loki to heel. Either way, you would think that the frost giants would give Asgard in general and me in particular a wide berth after that. But then, your kind has never been renowned for being quick of mind."

"Get him!"

Four of the giants ran toward Balder at once, and the brave one did almost pity their simplistic strategy. Even as the quartet of large creatures converged on a small target, Balder quickly dove away from his position, leaving the four giants to crash into each other, their massive heads colliding with those of their fellows.

As the foursome collapsed in a heap of cranial trauma, Balder turned his attention to the other two, which included the one who recalled his defeat of Utgard-Loki and the one who only growled.

The growler raised an axe and swung it directly at Balder's head with speed that belied his massive form. Balder heard the whistle of the axe's blade as he barely managed to dodge it.

However, the other giant rather sensibly tackled Balder with a low dive when he was in his crouch. Balder and the giant rolled about on the ground for several seconds before Balder was able to extricate himself.

Now Balder stood between the two giants, the growler with his axe and the other one with his great sword.

For several seconds, Balder managed to keep both at bay. He ducked the growler's axe and parried the other's sword, then kicked the growler in the shin followed by a strike at the other's side, barely parried in time by the great sword. He rolled between the growler's legs, thus avoiding a swing of the great sword, and keeping the axe from cleaving his head in twain.

A much louder growl, now, as the giant turned and swung his axe at Balder, but this time Balder raised his sword to parry the blow, rather than dodge it. The giant's growl was cut off by an "Arooo?" of surprise, as the axe slammed into Balder's sword with a bone-shuddering impact of metal on metal. The giant stared, transfixed. Every other time some fool had tried to parry his great axe with a sword, the sword had been shattered by the giant's sheer strength.

Until now.

Balder took advantage of the giant's shock to rear back and punch the creature in the stomach with his full strength. The growling giant fell to the ground, having lost the ability to catch his breath.

That left just the one with the great sword, who regarded Balder angrily. "What did you mean that we are not renowned for being quick of mind?"

Rather than respond verbally, Balder simply pressed the attack with his own sword. The giant parried with surprising skill. Indeed, each time Balder pressed his attack, the giant responded with a parry that Balder recognized as a formal move from his own training as a youth.

"I am impressed," he said to his opponent. "Most giants rely on their brute strength to win the day, yet you possess skill with a blade that rivals even my own!"

"Say instead that my skill surpasses yours, for I am Bjarni, son of Thjasse, great-grandson of Ymir himself, and from this day forth I shall be known as the one who killed Balder the Bra—"

The rest of Bjarni's rant was cut off as Balder smacked Bjarni on the side of the head with the flat of his blade.

Bjarni fell to the ground, stunned, both from the blow to his head and at not being able to fulfill what he had expected to be his destiny.

Balder looked about and saw that Sif was now being harried by several giants, and the ones the Warriors Three had taken on were similarly ganging up on the trio. Hrungnir himself was hanging back away from the fighting, but unable to proceed forward to Asgard due to the melee he had inspired.

Now that he had a moment to himself, however, Balder had a tactic he could employ. But before he could begin to do so, he heard a distant rumbling.

And then the ground shook beneath everyone's feet as the sound of thunder filled the air.

And then the sky crackled with lightning that flashed in everyone's eyes.

And then a red-and-blue figure flew upward into the sky and started hurtling toward the giants.

Goldfaxi reared back on his hind legs and gave a pitiful whinny at the display. Hrungnir had to struggle to maintain his grip upon the horse, his legs tightening around the horse's middle while his hands clutched the reins for dear life.

Thor rocketed through the air and smashed into Hrungnir, knocking the giant from his mount.

The giants all ceased what they were doing, stunned at seeing their leader brought low.

Thor came around for another pass. "Yield, Hrungnir, or face the wrath of a storm as only the god of thunder can rain down upon you!"

"Make it rain all you wish, Thor," Hrungnir bellowed over the sound of the precipitation crashing down upon the plain, "but I shall not rest until I have had my revenge! I have already had indignity rained upon me from Asgard, so let your storm fly! Asgard will be mine, and Odin's broken body will be laid at my feet!"

"I say nay," Thor cried. "I say *never*! Asgard shall not be yours as long as I draw breath!"

"Time to end your breathing, then." Hrungnir grinned and leapt back upon Goldfaxi.

Thor whipped 'round his hammer. More thunder roared. More lightning flashed. And more giants cringed.

Balder knew that the giants' shock could only make his plan a better one. Balder had often been called "the shining one," and those words were no mere poetry.

"Everyone," he cried out, "shield your eyes!"

And then Balder used his unique ability to glow brightly.

\* \* \*

Sif, Thor, and the Warriors Three all covered their eyes, while the frost giants felt the brightness even more than they were blinded by it. For Balder's brightness was that of the sun itself, and it was anathema to the frost giants, who preferred the chill of winter to the glow of summer that Balder's power provided.

Seeing what his dear friend had done, Thor immediately whirled his hammer as fast as he could over his head.

The thunder and lightning intensified more and began to strike the individual giants one by one.

Those frost giants who were not felled immediately ran out into the Ida Plain.

One of those was Hrungnir who, with a murderous look at the thunder god, kicked Goldfaxi into a gallop.

Again Thor whirled his hammer, but this time it was to have Mjolnir take him to the air again. Flying over the plain, he had a spectacular view of all the giants scattering to the winds, running toward the mountains at the far end of Ida. Ahead of all of them was Hrungnir atop Goldfaxi.

"Come storm!" Thor cried. "Obey your master, Thor, and strike at the varlets who would invade the glowing halls of Asgard! Strike! And do not cease until our enemies lie insensate at the feet of the god of thunder!"

Thor felt the power of the storm course through Mjolnir and through him. His birthright was to make the thunder and lightning obey him, and he gathered that power to him and let it loose through his hammer upon the Ida Plain.

Lightning cracked, thunder boomed, and rain fell from the

sky in sheets, pelting the giants and forcing them to their knees.

Sif, Balder, and the Warriors Three strode out into the plain, the rain rattling off their armor, and they gathered up the frost giants. Their foes whimpered, having been weakened by Balder's glow and frightened by Thor's might.

Thor landed alongside his friends and soon they had all the forlorn frost giants rounded up around the pile of more than half a dozen giants that had fallen as a result of Volstagg's fists.

And then he realized that one was missing.

"Where is Hrungnir?"

The others looked about, but the very storm that Thor had summoned had reduced visibility to almost nothing. The warriors of Asgard could barely even see the nearby mountains.

Thunder echoing behind her words, Sif said, "I do not see him, nor his gold-maned horse."

Thor shook his head. "Hrungnir's mount is second only to my father's own Sleipnir for speed. In truth he might easily have been able to outrun even this storm."

Fandral laughed, his well-kept blond hair now a dark brown and flat against his head from the rain. "What does it matter? We have taken Hrungnir's subjects!"

Volstagg added, "Hrungnir would be best to use his speedy horse to ride as far from Asgard as possible, lest he feel Volstagg's wrath as his fellows did."

"Yes," Sif said, "I doubt we will hear much from Hrungnir after this defeat."

Thor raised his hammer upright, and within moments the

storm dispersed, the rain slowed to nothing, and the sun started to shine again.

"Today is another victory, my friends! Let us bring these perfidious giants to Odin's dungeon. They shall enter the city gates, not as the invaders they had hoped, but as our prisoners. And then tonight—we feast!"

All five of Thor's fellow warriors cheered Thor as they led or carried the defeated giants to their fate.

# CHAPTER FIVE

"**H**ilde! Flosi's touching me!"

"Am *not*! I wouldn't *ever* touch *you*, Alaric!"

"Would too!"

Gunnhild, daughter of Volstagg, hated being called Hildy—that was a stupid little girl's name—but was willing to be called Hilde, a subtle but important difference. She rolled her eyes at the behavior of her younger siblings.

Mother and Frigga were taking the children of Asgard to a place in the Vale of Crystal to be safe in case the frost giants invaded. They had charged Hilde with keeping an eye on Alaric and Flosi, one of her younger brothers and one of her younger sisters, who had been fighting for *weeks*.

Because she was the oldest girl, Hilde was always stuck taking care of the babies when Mother was too busy. This once, Hilde didn't mind so much, since she knew it was important for everyone to behave, and—even with Frigga's help—Mother had her hands full with all the other children of Asgard.

This wasn't the first time this had happened. When Surtur attacked Asgard, Frigga had taken the children into the mountains to hide. Odin had told Hilde that he wanted the children to protect his wife, and Hilde had believed him at the time, but now that she was older and smarter, Hilde knew better.

She wondered if these frost giants were as dangerous as Surtur. She guessed they had to be, if Odin sent them all away again.

"Flosi, *stop touching me!*"

"I'm *not!*"

Hilde sighed. She, Flosi, Alaric, and the rest of Volstagg's children were in the middle of the pack. Mother led the way through the mountain path, which was covered in snow; on one side was a huge drop to the ground that got even bigger the farther along they went. At least the path was wide, and everyone was staying on the side of the path that had the mountain.

Frigga took up the rear, making sure that the ones in back didn't stray off the snow-covered path. She was armed, which was different from the last time. When they ran from Surtur, the queen of Asgard had not been armed. That worried Hilde that the threat of the frost giants might even be worse.

Then again, Odin had been lost in the battle against Surtur, and not restored to Asgard for some time. Maybe Frigga just wanted to be prepared for the worst this time.

"Hilde, make her stop touching me!"

"*I'm not touching you!* I wouldn't touch you if I had to touch you to stop Ragnarok!"

Hilde cried out, "Enough! If you two don't stop talking, I'll throw both of you over the mountain!"

"You wouldn't dare." Alaric tried to sound tough, but Hilde could tell that he was scared that she'd actually do it.

Flosi was more defiant. "She *won't*. Mother would never forgive her if she killed us."

"Oh really?" Hilde asked, fists clenched. "*I* think that Mother will be grateful to have two fewer mouths to feed, and two less people making noise all the time. Wanna see who's right?"

Both Flosi and Alaric gulped audibly and then kept walking without saying a word.

Hilde smiled. It was just a question of reasoning with the little ones.

They trudged through the snow a bit farther in lovely silence.

So of course, it couldn't last. Out of nowhere, Alaric asked, "What's that noise?"

"*Will* you be quiet?" Hilde said

But then Flosi said, "I hear it, too!"

Those two wouldn't even agree that the sky was blue, so if they each heard something, there probably was a noise.

And then Hilde heard it, too. It almost sounded like a horse galloping.

She turned and called back to the end of their group. "Lady Frigga! Do you hear that?"

Frigga, though, had already unsheathed her sword and was turning to see what might be making the sound—which was growing louder.

Hilde looked at the mountain side of the path and noticed that the rock of the mountain face was faceted and had plenty of handholds. Without another word, she started climbing.

"What are you doing?" Flosi cried out.

Alaric also yelled, "Hilde, that's crazy!"

Frigga heard the commotion and turned around to see Hilde clambering up the side of the mountain. "Hilde!"

At this point, however, Hilde had gotten far enough up the rock face to see some distance down the mountain.

Calling out to Frigga, she said, "There's a giant riding up the path! He's on a yellow horse!"

Frigga felt her heart grow cold. "Are you sure, Hilde?"

In fact, Hilde was completely sure, but it didn't do to question the mother of all Asgard, so Hilde squinted and peered down the mountain again.

"Definitely a big giant and definitely a yellow horse. Moving fast, too."

"Not good," Frigga muttered. "How far up the mountain has he come?"

"He just passed that weird tree that Kevin and Mick tried to climb."

Frigga nodded. The two mortal children whom Volstagg and Gudrun had adopted at Thor's request after their parents died on Midgard had immediately tried to climb the twisted oak near the base of the mountain, and it had taken quite a stern admonition from Gudrun to get them to cease. It had taken them half a day to traverse from that tree to where they were now. Hrungnir's mount would close that distance in much less time.

"Come down from there, Hilde, and gather everyone!"

"Okay!"

While Frigga wasn't entirely sure why Hrungnir would be riding alone through these mountains—there were better paths from Asgard to Jotunheim—the best reason she could think of was that Thor and the others had routed the giants, and Hrungnir took advantage of his mount's famous speed to escape.

It also explained why the giant had come this way. Were he endeavoring to escape her son's wrath at all costs, he would not have paid close attention to direction.

Sadly, that put the children right in his path. The very fate Odin had sent them into the mountains to avoid was now dangerously close to coming to pass.

"What is going on?" Gudrun asked.

Turning, Frigga saw that Hilde had indeed gotten everyone to stop moving and gather in one place.

"You must all move quickly. Hrungnir is on his way, and he must be stopped. You will all need to move twice as fast and hie yourselves to the Vale of Crystal."

"I don't understand," Gudrun said with a frown. "Hrungnir rides the fastest mount in the Nine Worlds, save only Odin's horse. Are we to outrun such a beast?"

"You will if I delay him. Go, Gudrun!" she added, holding up a hand to cut off another objection. "The more you speak, the greater chance that the giant catches you. When you enter the Vale of Crystal, you will be protected. But you must get there—now go!"

Gudrun harrumphed, but she was used to not getting a word in edgewise, having been married to Volstagg all these years. "Come, children, let us move quickly!" While Gudrun was a woman of some size, she also could be quite swift afoot when the need called for it—usually chasing one of the little ones around the house when they got into mischief—and so she immediately strode forward up the mountain path.

While she tried to set the pace, several of the children outstripped her, with Hilde naturally in the lead. She was physically the strongest of her children, even more so than the boys, and also the fiercest. Gudrun knew her daughter would not go too far ahead, lest they be separated, but she also felt that they were all a little bit safer with Hilde in the lead.

Behind them, Frigga watched as the children and Gudrun fled. Up to this point, they had been walking at a leisurely pace, not wishing to tire the children out—particularly Kevin and Mick, who were less hardy than Asgardian children, even though they had been dining on the golden apples of immortality since joining the family. But now that there was danger, she doubted anything would stop them from moving at top speed to the Vale of Crystal. Frigga herself had placed the wards upon the Vale that would protect all those who entered from any harm. She also would know when those wards were triggered, no matter where in the Nine Worlds she might be.

Frigga then proceeded back the way they had come. Best to be as far from the children as possible when she confronted Hrungnir. Besides, there was a plateau less than an hour's walk down the path that would be the perfect place to confront him and delay the giant until her charges were safe.

As she'd hoped, she reached that plateau before encountering Hrungnir, though the hoofbeats of Goldfaxi now echoed loudly through the chill air, signaling that the giant's arrival was imminent.

When Hrungnir turned 'round the bend and arrived at the plateau, he found himself confronted with fifty women wielding swords.

And all of them looked just like Frigga.

Yanking on the reins, Hrungnir cried, "Whoa!" The action was wholly unnecessary, as the sudden sight of a phalanx of Friggas was enough to spook the horse, and he stopped all on his own.

"Is it not enough that I am tormented by the husband? Now the wife vexes me!"

One of the Friggas said, "You will not pass this plateau, Hrungnir."

Another added, "We stand before you united."

A third said, "And we will not allow you through."

"Ha! First Odin had to disguise himself, then Thor uses that stupid hammer of his, and now you use illusions! You Asgardians are all illusions and shadows and toys with no true power. I will destroy each and every one of you!"

With that, Hrungnir kicked Goldfaxi forward and swung his club at the closest of the Friggas.

The club's impact caused the simulacrum Frigga had created to dissolve in a puff of light.

Frigga had hidden herself behind a snowdrift. Unfortunately, the illusions required proximity and effort to maintain. All she needed to do was keep throwing images of herself at the giant until Gudrun and the children made it safely to the Vale.

Luckily, Hrungnir had a very direct and deliberate approach. He simply attacked each image of Frigga in turn. It took him some time to wade through all fifty, especially once Frigga had them move about and dodge the giant's club, making him believe that *this* was the real one because it put up resistance.

In truth, when there were fifty, Frigga could do little but make them stand in a particular pose and speak with her voice, but once he eliminated a dozen or so, it freed her to manipulate the images more aggressively.

For Hrungnir's part, he had hoped that fighting fifty versions of Odin's wife and killing all of them would bring him the satisfaction that his abortive invasion of Asgard had failed to provide. But all it served to do was frustrate him even further.

And so with each image of Frigga he clubbed into nothingness, he got angrier and angrier.

Seeing the giant's fury, Frigga sent two of her illusory selves toward the edge of the plateau.

One held up her sword. "Face me if you dare, giant."

"Assuming you are not a coward," the other said, her sword lowered. "My husband has already defeated you, and it seems my son has done the same—so you come to run and hide in the mountains only to be beaten by me."

"Your husband tricked me! And you will pay for his perfidy,

woman!" Hrungnir shrieked as he kicked Goldfaxi into a gallop, rushing headlong toward the two illusions.

But then the horse pulled up, showing more sense than Hrungnir, skidding to a halt before both mount and rider could go tumbling over the edge.

The snow kicked up by Goldfaxi's sudden stop was enough to penetrate the spell, and the two Friggas by the edge also disappeared.

Hrungnir patted his noble horse on the side of the head. "Well done, my faithful steed. We would surely both have perished had I assaulted these false images." He dismounted from the horse and again patted him, this time on the side. "Rest, Goldfaxi, for I have taxed you much this day. I will deal with Odin's trollop myself."

A dozen images remained, and Frigga was starting to feel the stress of casting so many illusions at once. Still, she persevered, for the wards in the Vale had not yet been activated. And so the twelve Friggas moved to surround the giant.

Hrungnir held up his club and smiled. "I know you are nearby, witch. Even Loki could not work such magicks from a distance, and you are far from your son's equal in sorcerous matters."

"Oh, you believe that, do you?" said one of the Friggas.

Another said, "I taught my son everything he knows."

"But," a third said, "that doesn't mean I taught him everything *I* know."

A fourth Frigga moved to attack Hrungnir with her sword,

an obvious frontal assault that the giant easily parried, sending another simulacrum to oblivion.

But even as Hrungnir swung his club through the insubstantial form of Odin's wife, two more illusions attacked him from behind, and while the swords they carried had no physical substance, Frigga had imbued these final eleven images with magickal force that could be transmitted through the blades.

Hrungnir screamed as the swords of the two illusions sliced through his belly, weakening him with eldritch force. Snarling due to the unexpected pain, Hrungnir swung his club blindly behind him to eliminate those two, and then he charged at three more of them, wiping them out before they could raise their swords.

Of the half-dozen remaining, several managed to strike Hrungnir, but none were enough to fell the giant, and soon enough they had all been dispatched, leaving the frost giant to stand, weakened, but alone save for his mount.

"I know you're nearby, witch!" Hrungnir bellowed. "Do not think you can hide from me! I may not have your gift for spellcraft, but the frost giants are as one with the snow and ice, and none may hide amidst the cold from such as I for long."

And then Hrungnir upraised his arms, commanding the snow on the ground to move away and blow off the very same cliff's edge that Frigga tried to trick Hrungnir into going over.

Within moments, Frigga's cover was blown away, and she was forced to stand and face the giant.

"Your pretty tricks are at an end, wife of the hated All-Father. And without your illusions, you are nothing."

Frigga raised her sword. "Do you imagine, Hrungnir, that I am helpless before you? After all, you know that the mother of Loki is proficient in the ways of spellcraft. Does it not follow that the mother of Thor is able to fight?"

"Ha!" Hrungnir followed his derisive laugh with a mighty swing of his club.

One that Frigga easily parried with her sword. For while it was hardly the Sword of Frey, the wielder of which could never know defeat, Frigga's sword was fashioned for her by Eitri, the master smith of the dwarves. And so when the giant's club—made from the mighty oaks that had grown in Jotunheim since the dawn of time—collided with Frigga's blade, it echoed throughout the mountains.

Hrungnir expected that the Mother of Asgard would have a powerful blade, but he did not expect her to have the physical strength to withstand even a parried blow from a giant.

Frigga took advantage of the giant's shock by pressing her attack. Hrungnir parried each of her strikes, but it grew more difficult with each one. The magickal blows from the illusory swords added to the brutal attacks by Thor to wear away at even the frost giant's mighty constitution.

Unfortunately, Frigga herself was also growing weaker. It had been a very long time since she had cast so many spells at once. But still the wards had not been triggered, and until Gudrun and the children were safe, she dared not let up on her assault.

Frigga swung her sword at Hrungnir's left side. He blocked it, of course, but she immediately swung the sword over her head and down at the frost giant's right ankle. Hrungnir was able to dodge the strike by lifting his foot, which prompted Frigga to thrust the hilt of her sword at the giant's chest. With one foot off the ground, Hrungnir lost his balance and toppled backward, but he managed to shove at Frigga before falling, and she too wound up on her back in the snow.

Both of them quickly got to their feet, one feinting, the other parrying, with neither gaining an advantage.

"You fight well, Frigga," Hrungnir said, respecting his foe enough to use her name rather than an epithet. "Odin chose his wife well."

"What makes you think *he* chose *me*?" Frigga asked with a sweet smile, and then kicked a pile of snow upward toward the giant's face.

It only distracted the giant for but a moment, but it was enough for Frigga to come at him with her sword—

—or, rather, attempt to. She slipped on the very snow pile she had just kicked and stumbled forward, right into the grip of the giant.

Hrungnir wrapped both his meaty hands around Frigga's waist. "You fought well, Frigga. Though I am the victor now, know that—unlike your husband with his tricks and your son with his foolish hammer—I truly believe that you could have beaten Hrungnir the Mighty in a fair fight. Alas, the Nine Worlds are many things, but fair is not among them."

Barely able to catch her breath from being crushed by the giant, Frigga asked, "Am I to be killed, then?"

"Oh no, my worthy foe. You are of far more use to me alive than dead. No, you are a prisoner of the frost giants."

Even as consciousness fled from Frigga, she at last felt the activation of the wards that surrounded the Vale of Crystal.

Gudrun and the children were safe.

And then Frigga's mind went dark.

# CHAPTER SIX

The first thing Odin did when Thor returned to the throne room to announce that Hrungnir's forces were routed was to send his son to the Vale of Crystal to tell Frigga, Gudrun, and the children that they could return home.

"Perhaps I acted in haste to send them from the city," Odin said, "but I feared the wrath of Hrungnir might lead to the endangering of the innocents of Asgard. It is my sworn duty to protect them."

Thor smiled. "You need not explain, Father. Evil's strength is its lack of caring for the fate of those not involved in the conflict. While Hrungnir's animus is toward you, not the children, it would still be very much in his character to harm them to get to you. It was right that you sent them away." He knelt respectfully before the All-Father. "I will hie myself to the Vale of Crystal at once!"

After exiting the throne room, Thor whirled his hammer over his head, and then it shot into the air, pulling him along through the skies. He watched as the soldiers of Asgard brought the giants to the dungeon, joining Baugi the troll, who also dared to menace the great city. Then he flew leisurely toward the mountains.

Something caught his eye, and he cut short his flying to alight on a large plateau. The snow was heavily disturbed, and there were many scattered foot- and hoofprints, the former of two different sizes.

There had been a great battle on that spot, and it was recent. And this plateau was on the route Gudrun and Frigga would have taken to the Vale. It was unclear which of the two people walked away from the fight—the only prints that continued onward were those of the horse.

Again Thor twirled his hammer, but now he felt the need for haste. Urging Mjolnir to move at top speed, he flew to the Vale of Crystal. Located in the heart of the Asgard Mountains, the Vale was a dodecahedron made entirely of crystals. Mined millennia ago by the dwarves, the crystals were useful for the channeling of spells. The mages of Vanaheim traded the dwarves for the crystals and constructed this place. It had not had much use in a while, though Thor knew that his mother used to come here quite a bit, and also that she was capable of warding it against attack. No doubt, that was why the All-Father chose it as the place to hide the children of Asgard from the frost giants.

He alighted at the Vale's entrance—or, rather, where he was fairly certain the entrance was. Frigga had shown him the location of the hidden entrance once, and he recalled that all he needed to do was walk through.

Sure enough, he approached what appeared to be a solid wall of crystal and walked right through it to a large sitting room filled with chairs and tables and cushions.

The first words he heard upon entering were, "Frigga, you finally made it!"

Even as Gudrun said those words, Thor felt the impact of several small bodies on his legs.

"Thor!"

"Yay, it's Thor!"

"Is Asgard safe?"

"Are all the giants dead?"

Gudrun's words had given the thunder god pause, but he put on a smile for the benefit of the children. "Yes, Asgard is safe once more. Of the giants who attacked, only their leader Hrungnir got away. Rather than remain to face the consequences of his actions alongside his people, he turned and ran like the craven varlet he is."

Hilde—one of the few children not currently embracing Thor's calves—said, "We know, we saw him coming up the mountain. Frigga stayed behind to stop him."

"We thought you were her," Gudrun added. "She should have come here by now."

Anger boiled within Thor's heart. The mighty battle he saw the aftermath of on the plateau was almost certainly between Frigga and Hrungnir. Frigga, he knew, was on foot, and Hrungnir was riding the speedy Goldfaxi. Which meant that the fact that hoofprints were all that exited the battlefield bespoke a victory for the frost giant.

But he tamped down the anger, not wishing the children, or Gudrun, to worry. "I have come in Frigga's stead. The battle is won, and Asgard is safe once again. You may all return to your homes."

Gudrun let out a huge breath. "Thank the Fates. I feared we would be trapped in this crystalline labyrinth for weeks."

Thor chuckled despite himself. Gudrun hated being away from her own home. She often made excuses not to attend feasts in the great hall of Asgard, preferring to stay behind and keep an eye on the children too small to attend those feasts. While many teased Volstagg about how he went out on adventures with Fandral and Hogun to avoid being stuck at home with Gudrun, the truth, Thor knew, was that Gudrun herself was the one that preferred to remain alone, leaving the adventuring to her husband. A gentle home life was what she preferred.

Well, as gentle as possible with so many children underfoot.

Prying the children off his legs, Thor said, "I must return to Asgard immediately. The passage you came by is clear and safe—you may return at your leisure."

Gudrun favored him with a bright smile. "Thank you, Thor."

He bowed. "Of course, my lady Gudrun."

Only after he departed from the Vale and took to the air once more did he allow his concern to show on his countenance.

This battle with Hrungnir may have ended well for Asgard, but Thor now realized that the war with the giant had only just begun, and his foe had struck a brutal blow.

Upon returning to Asgard, he went straight to the throne room, where Odin was consulting with his vizier.

Odin saw his son enter, and dismissed the vizier, for they

were discussing minor matters of state that were of very little moment. He could postpone them to speak to his son, especially since he had returned so quickly from checking in on Frigga.

"I am afraid, Father, that I bring dire news." Quickly, Thor filled Odin in on what he had learned: that Gudrun and the children were safe, but Frigga was last seen going to engage Hrungnir.

"The children were well enough settled in that they had been at the Vale long enough for Mother to have joined them," Thor said, "*if* she had won her battle against Hrungnir. But the giant is a doughty warrior, whatever his flaws. Mother would be hard-pressed to be victorious against him."

For several seconds, Odin did not reply.

Then, without warning, he cried out with an incoherent scream as power flew forth from his fingertips, smashing several of the statues that dotted the throne room.

However, the outburst did little to assuage Odin's feelings on the subject. "I am a fool, Thor. I should have revealed myself to Hrungnir."

Thor shook his head. "That would have changed nothing, Father. Hrungnir's arrogance would have forced him to challenge Sleipnir even knowing that 'twas him and you rather than a stranger and an unknown horse."

"Perhaps, but I suspect the giant's attack was as much due to my deception as it was Sleipnir's victory over Goldfaxi. Had I but revealed myself—even after the race—then only I would have incurred Hrungnir's wrath. Instead, in my arrogance, I have caused the endangerment—possibly even the death—of the light of my very life."

The Warriors Three then came into the hall, accompanied by a strange creature that seemed to be dripping water.

Peering more closely, Thor saw that it was an ice elemental—a clump of ice given temporary form and substance. Such creatures were commonly employed as errand-makers in Jotunheim, but they did not survive for long outside the cold climes of the land of the giants.

"Forgive our intrusion," Fandral said, "but this messenger from Jotunheim was quite insistent upon an audience with Odin."

Odin sat down upon his throne, placing his hands firmly on the armrests. "You were correct to do so, Fandral. Bring him forward, ere he melts before speaking his piece!"

In the time it took for the creature to walk across the throne room, it became half a head smaller, its features less distinct, a trail of cold water left behind in its wake. Fandral, Volstagg, and Hogun walked alongside it, joining Thor at the foot of the throne.

The creature made a small bow to the throne before speaking. "Hail to Odin All-Father, king of the powerful gods of Asgard. I bring greetings from Hrungnir the Brawler."

"Arrive at the purpose of your journey quickly, messenger," Odin said in a grave, threatening tone.

Showing no signs of being so threatened, the creature continued. "The Lady Frigga is a guest of the mighty Hrungnir.

She is unharmed," the messenger added quickly, even as Odin leaned forward in his seat. "She will remain so, for Hrungnir has no quarrel with her. However, her release back to Asgard can be accomplished only one way: Thor Odinson must travel to Jotunheim *alone* and face Hrungnir in personal combat. It will be Hrungnir against Thor—neither may have assistance in any way from their fellows. If your son abides by these terms, then Frigga will be released back to you. If Thor does *not* abide by these terms—if, for example, another Asgardian comes with him or in his place—then Frigga's status as an unharmed guest of the frost giants will be rather negatively changed. If you accept, Thor must arrive in Jotunheim by nightfall. If Thor does not come alone, or does not come at all, then Frigga's life will come to a premature end."

And then the creature's entire body warped and melted; within seconds, there was but a puddle before the All-Father's throne.

"It would seem," Hogun said, "that the messenger was not instructed to wait for a reply."

Thor shook his head. "He will know his reply by whether or not I arrive alone in Jotunheim to face him."

Odin stared at his son with his one good eye. "Summon brave Balder and noble Sif to the throne room!"

Thor widened his eyes in surprise. It was unlike his father to consult with others on such a matter. His word was, after all, law.

Within moments, both had joined Thor and the Warriors

Three in the throne room. Thor quickly filled them in on the latest development.

When Thor finished, Odin said, "The decision before me is a difficult one, and while I typically would but *make* the decision and have done with it, I find now that concern for both my wife and my son do cloud my normally clear judgment. You are the finest Asgard has to offer, and so I ask of you: What do you recommend that Odin decide?"

Thor spoke before anyone else could. "You need not concern yourself with my own well-being, Father. Gladly will I face the giant in order to save Mother—or indeed even were her life not at stake. He has already escaped once."

"Thor is correct," Fandral said, "but he should not go alone. Even if the Lady Frigga were not his prisoner, it would behoove us to seek out Hrungnir and smite him for daring to invade."

"Agreed," Sif said. "One good invasion deserves another. We can have troops gathered within a day, and we will ride across the Ida Plain, through the mountains, and into Jotunheim. We will rout them, and take Frigga home after our triumph."

Volstagg nodded his round head. "Indeed! Why, simply allow the Lion of Asgard to march through Jotunheim, and the frost giants will be cowed by my magnificence!"

"Cowed with laughter, more like," Hogun muttered. "I respectfully disagree with my comrades, Lord Odin. Hrungnir does not strike me as one who goes back on his word. If any other than Thor approach, the Lady Frigga's life would be forfeit."

Balder nodded. "I agree with Hogun. Hrungnir is bold and fearless. And from what I hear, he has encroached quite heavily on Nornheim." Balder spoke obliquely, though it was hardly a secret that Karnilla, the Queen of the Norns, loved Balder, and that the brave one had taken to returning the favor. Still, Balder knew his friends disapproved of the liaison—they did not know the Norn Queen as he did—and so he spoke directly of it as little as possible.

Thor looked over his dearest friends. "My brave and noble comrades, I do appreciate your willingness to join me in Jotunheim, but Hogun and Balder are correct. For Mother's sake, I *dare* not do aught but go alone to face Hrungnir as he has requested."

Angrily, Sif asked, "And what proof have we that he will keep his word that he will fight you alone?"

"He will keep his word," Odin said. "Whatever else Hrungnir may be, he is no oath-breaker. He proved that to me when we raced, for he thought me a simple traveler and could easily have gone back on the wager. But he did not. And Balder is correct— I encountered him on the road that leads from Nornheim to Jotunheim. If he is bold enough to challenge both Karnilla and myself, then he is not one to be trifled with—particularly with Frigga's life at stake."

Sif, however, was not convinced. "He is still a frost giant. Perhaps he was willing to keep his word regarding a simple horse race, but now? He has been humiliated before his subjects— first by Sleipnir showing up his precious mount, and then by his failed invasion of Asgard. In order to win back their love and affection after so thorough a defeat as we handed him, he will need to do something bold. Obviously, he wishes to be the one to finally defeat Thor, but I'm sure he will settle for being the one to kill Frigga if he must."

"You speak wisely, Sif," Odin said, "and your words do give me pause—but no more than that." He rose to his feet once more. "Thor will go alone, and he will do battle with Hrungnir. So be it!"

Thor bowed. "As you command, Father."

"However," Odin added quickly, "Hrungnir requested only that Thor go to Jotunheim alone to face the giant in battle. He said nothing of what we might do here in Asgard. Balder, Sif, you and the Warriors Three will gather our forces on the Ida Plain. Summon Harokin and have him muster the Einherjar as well. Should Thor fall, or should Hrungnir become as poor at keeping his word as Sif fears, then the entire wrath of Asgard will be brought to bear on Jotunheim, and the frost giants will rue the day they ever left the cold confines of their land."

The five of them all bowed their heads. Balder said, "It will be done, Lord Odin."

Stepping down from the throne, Odin put his hands on Thor's shoulders. "I wish you well, my son. The life of your sweet mother—my noble wife—hangs in the balance. But I have ever relied upon your strong right arm and your ability to wield Mjolnir to defend all the Nine Worlds. I am sure you will do no less on this day."

"You may be assured, Father, that I would face Hela herself if it meant saving Mother's life." With that, Thor turned and left the throne room, his friends on his heels.

Balder patted Thor on the back. "Fight well, my friend. I wish I could go with you—but if Frigga is to be saved, I do believe that you have by far the best chance of doing so."

"Thank you, my old friend."

"Be wary, son of Odin," Hogun said. "Hrungnir did come upon Asgard more quickly than he should have before Heimdall's sharp eyes saw him. He may have aid in his campaign against us."

"You may well be correct, Hogun," Thor replied with a nod, "but it matters not. The life of my mother is all with which I am concerned this day. All I care for with regards to Hrungnir is how I may defeat him."

"And defeat him, you shall," Fandral said with his trademark grin. "I am sure of it!"

Volstagg added, "Indeed!" with a pat on Thor's back that, unlike the softer one from Balder, threatened to crack the thunder god's spine. Thor stumbled a bit forward as Volstagg added, "The only way you could be guaranteed victory is if I were to accompany you, of course, but failing that, I'm sure you'll do well on your own."

Thor couldn't help but laugh. Volstagg always knew how to disarm his foes and cheer his friends with his boasts. "Many thanks, my corpulent friend."

The Warriors Three and Balder went off to summon

Harokin, the leader of the Einherjar. The warriors of Valhalla were the greatest of the dead heroes of Asgard, gathered into a single fighting force, and there were few better to have at one's back in war.

However, Sif remained behind.

At first, they simply regarded each other. They had been through much, these two, as warriors, as friends, and as more than friends. Much was said with only an expression, and Thor knew just from Sif's eyes that she was concerned for the safety of both him and his mother.

"Be wary, Thor. I hope Odin is right—but I fear *I* am."

"It matters little, Sif, for I must fight either way. But if I am triumphant over Hrungnir, then it will matter even less, for the giant will be defeated once and for all and Frigga will be returned to us."

Sif smiled. "Be swift and brave, Thor—and if you should fall, be assured that all of Asgard will avenge you."

Thor gave her a small smile. "I'm sure that will comfort me on my way to Valhalla. Now stand you back."

As Sif moved backward, Thor again twirled his hammer, preparing himself for his journey.

To the skies, he cried, "Be you alert, Hrungnir, for the thunder god comes to face you for your final reckoning!"

And then, accompanied by the crash of thunder, he took to the skies and headed for Jotunheim.

# CHAPTER SEVEN

Loki had observed the entirety of the battle on the Ida Plain with a combination of amusement and frustration.

The amusement was mostly at the expense of the frost giants themselves. While he had no great love for the denizens of Asgard, he had even less for those of Jotunheim. Laufey hid his son, ashamed of his tiny stature, and would have rather he died—though the giant could not bring himself to do the deed himself. Instead, after defeating Laufey, Odin took the giant-king's child in and raised him as his own.

Loki had, in truth, hoped for more from his blood relations. At the very least, he'd hoped they would get as far as the trolls did, but the trickster did underestimate Heimdall.

And perhaps he overestimated the giants in general and Hrungnir in particular. The Brawler had gained an outsized reputation as the latest of the gang leaders who had tried to rally the frost giants to his banner. Loki was beginning to think that Hrungnir's legend was entirely an artifact of the animal between his legs rather than the brain between his ears.

Obviously, Loki was going to have to help his cousin.

Hrungnir had retreated from the battle on that speedy horse of his, an act of cowardice that Loki had to admit to admiring, and Loki decided to follow him, to give him a piece of his mind, since the giant had so little a mind of his own.

Unfortunately, the journey proved more problematic than Loki had anticipated, as he had decided to do as Hrungnir did and take the most direct route to Jotunheim, through the mountains. Last time he'd taken the more circuitous route Odin had followed, via the Sea of Marmora, which was on level ground. But while the mountainous path was far more direct, it was also far colder, and Loki had reckoned without the nature of the shape he had assumed. Insects avoided winter climes for a reason, after all.

Struggling to stay aloft in the frigid air, Loki alighted in a crevasse that he hoped Heimdall wasn't keeping a close eye on. Once there, he transformed himself into a wolf.

However, while the lupine form with its greater mass and coat of fur provided more protection from the chill, even at a full gallop, a wolf could not progress through the mountains as quickly as an airborne creature like the fly.

For a brief moment, Loki toyed with the notion of simply teleporting, but that was an expenditure of magickal power he dared not indulge in. The simulacrum at his keep was complex and needed to be mentally maintained constantly in order to continue to fool Heimdall. And while the guardian of Asgard might not take notice of a crevasse in the mountains, he would surely discover if there was a hint that the sleeping figure in Loki's bed was anything other than Loki.

And so Loki took the time to lope through the mountains.

As he did so, he formulated the plan by which he would ensure that Hrungnir would, at least, put up a decent fight.

Eventually, the wolfen form of Loki arrived at Hrungnir's redoubt on the outskirts of the frigid lands. It was a massive stone structure that seemed hastily put together. It had none of the elegance of the stone castles that many other giants favored, but Hrungnir spent so much time away from it on his horse, Loki supposed he shouldn't have been surprised that he gave so little thought to the architecture of his headquarters.

Thjasse, Hrungnir's lieutenant—whom, Loki realized, had not gone on the campaign against Asgard—spied him as he approached the battlements and cried out, "Wolf!"

Through the wolf's snout, Loki said, "No wolf am I, but Loki, returned to speak to Hrungnir of his failure—and how it may be changed into a victory."

"Really?" Thjasse sounded dubious.

"Yes. I would speak with the mighty one."

Before Thjasse could say anything, Hrungnir stepped out through the giant doorway that provided ingress to the redoubt. "So, the trickster has returned. Good, because I would have words with Loki."

"And I you," Loki said with a snarl. "You made, if you'll pardon the expression, a gigantic mess of this."

"*I* have?" Hrungnir raised his arms as if to pound the wolf. "It was *Loki* who gave us a route that would take us *into* Asgard, not to an ambush on the Ida Plain!"

"It is true that Heimdall spotted you sooner than expected,

but still and all, you are frost giants! A gang of idiot trolls managed to do better against Thor and his comrades than you were able to accomplish. Had you not Goldfaxi to enable your retreat, you would be alongside your fellows in the dungeons below the Realm Eternal."

"And had I not Loki to 'aid' me—"

Loki interrupted, "You wouldn't have gotten as far as the Ida Plain. Do not be foolish, Hrungnir. You need me—apparently, even more than I believed." Loki then whispered the conclusion of the spell he had begun upon departing the mountains.

A mighty wind started to blow, gathering up the stones from the very ground around them. The wind whirled faster into a devastating funnel, but it swept up only the rock and earth around them. The snow and plants on the ground, even the hair on the heads of the giants, remained undisturbed by the currents.

With a mighty crack, the rock pieces slammed into each other, merging and forming a bipedal structure.

When the wind died down, the giants saw before them a giant-sized suit of stone armor. And beside it a massive club.

"Both the armor and the weapon are enchanted. No force may be brought against them that would cause them to be damaged. Even Thor's hammer would be unable to shatter the stone. So when next you invade Asgard—"

"There shall be no invasion of Asgard."

That brought Loki up short. "Whyever not? Has Odin's offense been eliminated? Has Hrungnir decided that being humiliated is *not* an affront that should be answered?"

"Oh, the affront will be answered, worry not. I have simply chosen a different path to achieve justice for Odin's insult. Even as we speak, Thor is wending his way to Jotunheim to do battle with Hrungnir in one-on-one combat."

Surprised, Loki asked, "And Thor agreed to this?"

"We will know soon enough. If he does not arrive by nightfall, then I will have to kill our guest."

"Guest?"

"A hostage from Asgard, whose life I am trading for battle with the thunder god. And now, thanks to you, I have the means to ensure victory!"

Thjasse then spoke. "Assuming Loki is amenable to your using his gifts to kill his adoptive brother."

"I believe I already addressed that particular concern, Thjasse. However, I will reiterate that I have no issue with Hrungnir being the cause of Thor's demise. My path to rule Asgard is blocked by both Odin and Thor. If Hrungnir removes Thor from the playing field, then my task is halved." He loped over to the stone armor in his lupine form. "So please, accept these gifts, and use them to win your battle with Thor."

"Excellent!" Hrungnir threw his head back and laughed. "This will be a battle for the ages! They will write of it in legend and song—and that song shall be 'The Death of Thor'!"

Loki was grateful that he was in wolfen form, as it meant the sigh of annoyance he let loose at Hrungnir's boast came out more like a snarl.

"Let me try this magickal armor you have provided, then."

Hrungnir walked over to the armor, and then hesitated, unsure of how to proceed.

"Merely touch it and it will encase you."

Hrungnir hesitated. "This is not a trick? Odin *is* still your father, and you *are* still the trickster. This may be a ploy to trap me within this statue you have magicked up."

"Technically, because he took me from your uncle, Odin can be considered my father, by default, I suppose. But do not believe that I have any filial regard. You may rest assured that there are no tricks here. If you are to fight Odin's other son, then I am here only to help. Touching that armor will place it around you, and you will be invulnerable."

With a chortle, Hrungnir said, "Excellent. My victory over Odin's favorite son is assured!"

Loki winced. It was certainly true that Thor was Odin's favorite. This never made any sense to Loki, as you would think a leader such as Odin would value brains and cunning over brute force. Not to mention that he was stuck with Thor as his son no matter what—he had *chosen* Loki. And yet he was still treated like this . . .

Yes, it would definitely be worthwhile to watch Hrungnir thrash Thor for the sins of their father.

Hrungnir stood by the stone armor that looked like a sculpture the giants had placed on their lawn. At first, he simply stared at it. It wasn't a solid piece of stone, he realized. The arms, legs, headpiece, and chestpiece were all separate, but linked together. The headpiece included a square gap for the giant's face.

Then the giant reached out to touch the armor, as instructed.

As Loki and the other giants watched, Hrungnir's body seemed to grow insubstantial, turned transparent, and then was sucked into the armor.

The other giants immediately tensed. Several of them raised their weapons.

Thjasse turned to face Loki. "What did you do?"

But then Hrungnir's face was visible in the gap in the helmet.

Cautiously, Thjasse turned again, this time to face his leader. "Hrungnir?"

Hrungnir raised an arm experimentally. Then he broke into a huge grin and reached down to pick up the enchanted club.

"Are you well, Hrungnir?" Thjasse asked, still sounding concerned.

"'Well?' Oh, Thjasse, I am far more than 'well.' With this armor surrounding me I am stronger than ever!"

Loki's wolfen snout curled back to bare his teeth, the closest he could come to a smile in this form. "You should test the armor's mettle."

Hrungnir tried to nod his head, though that was a difficult gesture in the armor. He turned to his fellow giants. "Attack me!"

The giants exchanged glances for a moment. True, giants sparred with each other all the time, and even Hrungnir engaged in those bouts from time to time, but those were mostly wrestling matches.

"I said, *attack!*"

Three of the giants raised their weapons and came at Hrungnir.

First, Arnborn swung at Hrungnir with his club. The weapon bounced off Hrungnir's side, and Arnborn was devastated to see a crack now running down the middle. "I've had this club since I was a boy!"

Next, Olav came at Hrungnir with his axe raised over his head. It came smashing down on the armor's helm, and splintered in twain, the axe head flying off into the snow, leaving Olav standing, stunned, with only the haft. "I stole this axe from a dwarf! It never even needed to be sharpened!"

And then Niels thrust his great sword right at Hrungnir's chest. The sword shattered upon impact. Niels then shrugged. "Never liked that sword, anyhow."

Hrungnir brayed a laugh to the very sky. "None shall be able to defeat me now!"

Thjasse, however, was more cautious. "We know that you cannot be harmed by even the finest weapons." He glanced at Niels. "Or the poorest. But fighting is offensive as well as defensive. Can you even move about in that thing?"

Hrungnir immediately strode across the snow to grab Arnborn. He moved remarkably swiftly for a person encased in stone, and he picked up a surprised Arnborn and tossed him aside.

"And your strength?" Thjasse asked.

Loki was starting to grow weary of Thjasse's skepticism. "The armor obviously does what I promised. Why must you—?"

"Because even Loki's truths are lies," Thjasse said.

Bridling at the interruption, Loki said, "That doesn't even make sense."

"No," Hrungnir said, "my lieutenant speaks true. Thjasse is clever and wise. I must know how strong I am now."

"The oak," Thjasse said immediately.

Hrungnir grinned. "Yes!"

The giants all moved to the rear of the redoubt. Loki followed on all fours, curious as to what oak they were speaking of.

Around back, they came upon a giant, grizzled oak tree. It had no leaves on it, and Loki soon realized that the tree was petrified.

Looking more closely, the trickster saw that the oak had scarring and markings all over it.

"This oak," Hrungnir said as he strode toward it, "has been the test of strength for my people for generations. Many giants have strengthened themselves against its unforgiving bark, but it has remained standing—it has remained unyielding." He pointed at one scar. "I remember my father making this very dent upon the tree. He said it was the mightiest blow he ever struck."

Hrungnir then reared back with a cocked fist and slammed it into the oak, shattering it into a million pieces.

The sundering of the petrified wood echoed throughout Jotunheim. Loki imagined that they heard the sound in all Nine Worlds, vibrating through the tendrils of Yggdrasil.

As the sound from the tree's destruction started to fade, a preternatural quiet spread throughout the area around Hrungnir's redoubt. Loki looked around and saw that the giants were all staring at the tree's remains in abject shock, their mouths hanging open. Flies could have entered their mouths unmolested, if it had not been too frigid for them.

Then, after several interminable seconds when Loki feared he was going to have to check to see if the giants were still alive, Hrungnir started to laugh.

Only then did the other giants join in, and soon the echoes of petrified wood being splintered were replaced by the echoes of braying laughter from a dozen or more frost giants.

"Oh, well done, Loki! This armor will ensure my victory over the thunderer! And after I have trounced him, then I will lead my forces back to Asgard! Armed as I am with this armor of yours, none shall be able to stop me. The broken bodies of Sif, Balder, the Warriors Three, Heimdall, and all the other puny gods will litter the path to Odin, where I will crush his one-eyed head on his very throne!" He faced his subjects and raised both hands in the air. "Victory!"

The giants all shouted, "Victory!"

Loki muttered, "You haven't won anything yet, fool," but his lupine voice could not be heard over the shouting.

Instead, he loped quietly toward the redoubt. Hrungnir mentioned a hostage, and Loki was curious as to whom the giant had kidnapped in order to bend Thor to his will.

# CHAPTER EIGHT

Normally, when Thor was carried through the heavens by Mjolnir, the hammer's speed was more than sufficient.

But now, as he rocketed over the mountains toward Jotunheim, it felt agonizingly slow.

While he always felt heavily the responsibility of protecting both Asgard and Midgard, it was as nothing compared to the responsibility he felt toward Frigga.

Strictly speaking, Frigga was not Thor's mother, for Thor had been born of a union between Odin and Jord, whom some mortals called Gaea, the earth-goddess of Midgard. Thor had always assumed that his affinity for the world of mortals was at least in part due to that particular quirk of parentage.

But while Jord was the woman who bore him, it was Frigga who raised him. Odin could charitably be called a distant father, if for no other reason than his responsibilities as All-Father took up a great deal of his time. And often his love for his son had to be tempered by his need to be a fair and stern ruler of all Asgard.

So it was Frigga who took care of him. Frigga who fed him and clothed him.

Frigga who told him all those stories: of Odin and his

brothers Vili and Ve, of his father's battle against Laufey that cemented Asgard's dominance over the frost giants, of her own marriage to Odin that united the Aesir and the Vanir under Asgard's banner.

Frigga who tended the injuries of the rambunctious child who was constantly getting into mischief—both due to his own headstrong nature and due to encouragement by a most pernicious-minded adopted brother.

Frigga who comforted Thor when he was sad, laughed with him when he was happy, and helped him when he was confused.

Frigga who taught Thor to read, who taught Thor to think, and perhaps most importantly, taught Thor compassion. For while he learned about how to make the hard choices a ruler needed to make from Odin, it was from Frigga that he learned the need to leaven those decisions with kindness and thoughtfulness.

Frigga who accepted no credit for her own work in keeping Asgard safe and as peaceful as possible, given that they were surrounded by foes. Never did she allow herself to be considered one of the leaders of Asgard, though she performed a leadership role—including today. She accepted the responsibility, but shied away from the power.

Thor owed his physical strength and command over the storm to Odin. He owed his heroism to Frigga.

And now he felt as though he had failed her. True, Thor and the others were able to defeat the frost giants, but Hrungnir had gotten away, and that set in motion the events that led to Frigga being his prisoner.

Against the trolls, Thor had taken it upon himself to fight Baugi, for Baugi was the leader.

Against the frost giants, he had allowed others to get in the way, and Hrungnir escaped. He had focused on the entirety of the giants rather than Hrungnir himself. He should have left the other giants to his comrades and focused on the leader as he had with Baugi, but Hrungnir's mighty blow with his club had angered the thunder god.

When he was a youth, Thor regularly let his temper get the best of him. Young Loki often took advantage of that to provoke Thor for some prank or other. As he grew older, that temper combined with his strength and the power of Mjolnir to blossom into arrogance. It was what led Odin to change Thor's shape to that of a crippled mortal and leave him trapped, amnesiac, on Midgard to teach him humility.

While those lessons were well learned, there were times when Thor still let his arrogance get the better of him. He thought he could take on all the frost giants himself, rather than let his friends do so while he focused on Hrungnir.

And Frigga had paid the price for his allowing Hrungnir to escape.

Based on what Gudrun had said, Frigga had deliberately engaged Hrungnir so that Volstagg's wife and the children of Asgard would be safe. It was exactly that selflessness that Thor tried every day to emulate.

Today, he had failed. And he would not let it stand.

He soon arrived over Jotunheim, and quickly sighted Hrungnir's keep. It was a flimsy redoubt, and Thor had to admit to disappointment. He recalled the grand halls of Utgard-Loki and Ymir and even that of Laufey, the first victim of Mjolnir when Odin wielded the hammer before gifting it to his son. They were halls worthy of a leader.

This was not. Hrungnir's keep was barely a habitable structure. Thor realized that Hrungnir's reputation was built primarily on the speed of Goldfaxi. He was beginning to believe that the giant had come to resemble his mount, specifically its backside.

And then he saw the giants gathered around what appeared to be a statue.

As he alighted upon the ground, Thor saw the statue move, and realized that it was stone armor. Hrungnir's face was visible underneath the helm.

"Is this, then, how you face me, Hrungnir? Hiding behind stone raiments?"

"No more than you hide behind your own armor, thunder god. Do you not wear a helmet to protect your head? Mail to protect your chest?"

"Very well, Hrungnir, if you feel you must use armor to face me, then so be it! But first, I demand proof of life!"

The giant frowned. "I beg your pardon?"

Thor shook his head. "You *claim* to have my mother as your prisoner. I would have you back your claim with action and show me that the Lady Frigga is alive and well and in your care."

Hrungnir stared angrily at Thor for many seconds before finally saying, "Do you doubt my word, thunder god?"

"I do indeed. Odin claims that you are no breaker of oaths, but I have difficulty putting stock in the honor of one who bargains with the life of a wife and mother."

"Very well. Thjasse!"

Thjasse stepped forward. "Shall I bring the woman out?"

"Yes." Hrungnir was, as usual, pleased with Thjasse's cleverness.

Within moments, Thjasse had disappeared into the keep, and returned with Frigga. Her hands and mouth were bound, preventing her from weaving any spells that might aid in her escape. Thor cursed Hrungnir for his perspicacity.

"As you can see, Thor, your mother is unharmed. The bindings are necessary to ensure her remaining our guest."

"Hostage, you mean," Thor said.

"Take her away," Hrungnir said, and Thjasse quickly moved to obey his wishes, bringing Frigga back into the keep.

The leader of the frost giants then turned to face Thor. "Your father spoke the truth about me. As proof I offer the fact that I did *not* kill him where he stood after his mount defeated mine in a foot race. I promised him safe passage away from us if he won, and I granted him that. Indeed, when last I encountered the All-Father, it was *he* who lied, *he* who deceived! He gave his name as 'Bolverk,' and did not identify his horse as the great Sleipnir. So do not speak to me of honor, thunderer—the frost giants of Jotunheim know the meaning of that word far more than you Asgardians do."

"Your words do you more credit than your actions, Hrungnir."

"Then hear these words, Thor! We will fight—you against me. None of my subjects will aid me in battle against you, and none of your oafish comrades will aid you in battle against me. It shall be the god of thunder versus the mighty brawler. The only way you may win the Lady Frigga's freedom is by defeating me!"

"Then stand fast, Hrungnir, for defeat you, I shall! None may harm the personage of the mother of all Asgard without paying the price, and you may rest assured that the cost I exact will be most dear!" He twirled the hammer over his head and threw it at Hrungnir's armored form, grabbing hold of the strap as he did so. As he rocketed toward his foe, he cried, "For Asgard! For Odin! And most of all, for Frigga!"

And then Thor crashed into Hrungnir's stone armor with a bone-shaking impact that slammed through the thunder god and sent him sprawling to the ground.

Hrungnir himself had not budged. Thor felt a most unaccustomed pain all up and down his body, particularly in his arms, which were what hit Hrungnir's stone armor the hardest.

"What sorcery is this?" Thor asked.

"Does it matter? It is *my* sorcery because *I* use it." Hrungnir punctuated his reply with an uppercut at Thor's prone form.

The punch collided with Thor's jaw and sent the thunder god through the air toward the keep. So stunned was he by the impact that he let go of Mjolnir as he sailed over the cold ground and landed in the snow.

Propping himself upright, Thor said, "Not since last I fought the Hulk have I been struck by so great a blow!"

Hrungnir started running toward Thor, his footfalls shaking the very ground. "Allow me to surpass it, then!"

And again, Hrungnir bent low and threw an uppercut, one that sent Thor hurtling to the sky, along with a dusting of snow.

Ignoring the ache in his ribs, Thor reached out at the apex of his impromptu flight. Mjolnir flew into his hand, and he used it to stay aloft.

But Hrungnir was now reaching down to the ground to pick up his club, which he then threw right at Thor. The weapon was not usually one that would be thrown, but it flew like a missile through the air. Thor was barely able to dodge it by flying downward, back toward Hrungnir.

Since the giant used his club the way Thor used his hammer, he decided to return the favor, and he swung Mjolnir like a club, striking Hrungnir in the side of the head.

It had no effect.

Hrungnir reached out and grabbed Thor's arms and tossed him aside, sending the thunder god skidding through the snow.

The club fell back to the ground with a muted thud, and Hrungnir trudged over to retrieve it. "And so it ends, son of Odin." He walked over to Thor's prone form and upraised the club. "Now you die."

Hrungnir swung downward toward Thor's head, intending

to smash the thunderer's face in. He would be known through-out all history as the one who finally destroyed Thor.

But just as the club was about to strike, Thor reached up with his hands and caught it.

"I say nay!" Thor cried as he pushed back against the club's momentum.

Hrungnir's surprise at Thor's actions led the giant to relax his grip for but a second, yet it was enough for Thor to use all his strength to push the club away. Hrungnir stumbled back-ward a few steps, allowing Thor to clamber unsteadily to his feet.

The battle had only just begun, and Thor already felt as if he'd been fighting the Hulk for several hours. He'd had many brawls with the gamma-irradiated brute over the years, starting from the earliest days of the Avengers, and Hrungnir's blows were very much like those of the green monster.

But the primary difference between the jade giant and the frost giant he now faced was that the Hulk grew stronger as he grew angrier. The first time Thor and the Hulk clashed in the caves of Gibraltar, Thor had almost lost due to that particular quirk.

He knew, however, that Hrungnir operated with no such advantage. Indeed, anger would no doubt reduce Hrungnir's capabilities in battle.

And so Thor once again took to the skies as Hrungnir got his bearings.

"You speak of honor, foul Hrungnir, yet you use magic to bolster your prowess."

"How dare you!" Hrungnir bellowed. "I no more hide behind this armor than you do behind that absurd hammer of yours!"

"It is no secret that one who challenges Thor does also challenge Mjolnir. The two names are fair intertwined in the minds of all who know of me throughout the Nine Worlds. But when those same folk do speak of Hrungnir—if, indeed, they speak of you at all—their words ring out regarding Goldfaxi and his speed. A challenge against you is considered a challenge against *your* might, or the fleetness of your horse's hooves—*not* against magickal armor."

"It is also no secret that Thor wielded a sword before Odin granted him possession of Mjolnir. I'm sure the foes you faced in battle after being gifted that hammer were similarly caught unawares. Did it stop you from thrashing them?"

Thor smiled. "It did not. But then, they were also not foolish enough to give the god of thunder time to catch his breath after a pounding."

And then Thor raised up his arms and summoned the storm that was his to control. Lightning crackled through the sky overhead, one of the bolts striking the top of the giant's lowly keep.

Hrungnir laughed. "Do you truly believe that your puny lightning can hurt me where your fists could not?"

"Your assumption, foolish Hrungnir, is that the lightning will be brought to bear on you."

And then several bolts of lightning struck not Hrungnir, but rather the ground near the giant's feet.

The lightning turned the snow into gas instantly, even as it ripped through the dirt beneath, vaporizing it until Hrungnir no longer stood on steady earth.

Waving his arms in a futile attempt to maintain his balance, Hrungnir suddenly was painfully aware of how heavy his new armor was. He fell backward and landed flat on his back, momentarily helpless.

Thor pressed his advantage, knowing it would not last. He flew down to the ground and pounded on Hrungnir's armor with Mjolnir.

Many of the giants present thought they would never hear a sound as loud and horrible as that of the petrified oak shattering from Hrungnir's mighty blow, but they were now proven wrong. That was as a whisper in the wind compared to the noise that resulted from Thor's hammer striking Hrungnir's armor.

The very ground did shake like that of a rampaging beast. Stones loosened in the giants' redoubt, and a nearby evergreen tree almost uprooted from the violent impact. Many of the giants who were close to the battle doubled over from the pain in their ears, so great was the sound.

Inside the keep, Frigga was being held in a large room that had furnishings of great size, none of which she could actually reach. Thjasse had placed her near some oversized chairs, guarded by a single giant. That guard took up a position at the room's only window, which afforded him a lovely view of the battle. Said window was too high to be of any use to Frigga, though she could hear the sounds of the clash.

When Mjolnir struck the magic armor, the impact of uru

against enchanted stone was enough to cause Frigga to fall over, unable to maintain her footing, bound as she was. Her guard also lost his footing, but he recovered more readily, using the windowsill to steady himself. Upon noticing that Frigga had fallen, he made no move to help her, but simply chortled.

"So much for the heartiness of the Asgardians. Can't even keep your feet."

Were she not gagged, Frigga would have reminded the brute that her hands were bound, but even if she had been able to speak the words, it would likely have had little effect.

Then again, if she had been able to speak, she would have uttered a spell that would have removed her from this place. Her battle against Hrungnir had drained her considerably, and she was not yet at anywhere near her full strength, but she would, at least, have been able to send herself a league or two away from this keep, enough to give her a head start.

Although at this point, she suspected, it did not matter. Just the fact that Frigga had been taken had been enough to rile her son, she had been able to see that much during her brief sojourn out of doors. Even if Frigga were able to effect an escape, it would change nothing. She would not be able to make it all the way to Asgard to inform Odin that she was safe, which would enable him to send the entire forces of Asgard to take on Hrungnir and his minions.

Of course, if she were free, she could, at the very least, aid Thor, since the terms of the battle relied upon Frigga being Hrungnir's prisoner.

And Thor would need all the help he could get, for Frigga could sense the power emanating from Hrungnir's new armor. She wondered whence he received it, though she feared she could make a rather educated guess that was very close to her own home . . .

Falling down from the impact of Thor's strike had proffered one advantage upon her: The gag that the giants had placed on her was now directly between her head and the floor of the keep. Rubbing her head against the floor caused the gag to shift. With a bit of patience, she might be able to eventually slide it off.

Luckily for her, the guard evinced no interest in actually paying attention to her. He was back to watching the battle.

Thor's blow was sufficiently powerful that it affected its wielder as much as it did his surroundings. The very force of his strike sent the thunder god head over heels across the snow-covered ground.

For several precious seconds, Thor was dazed, but he forced his wits to focus, forced his limbs to pay attention to his wishes, and he got to his feet.

To his horror, Hrungnir was doing the same.

Initially, Thor feared that his blow had been for naught, if the frost giant could so easily regain his feet, but the armor allowed Hrungnir's face to be seen, and that betrayed the truth. His visage showed strain and fatigue, and Thor knew then that his blow was not in vain.

But it was also not likely to be repeated. Thor's very limbs felt as if they were made of rubber; his bones felt as fragile as they had once been made by a spell of Hela's. On that occasion, he had had to fashion special armor to protect himself very much like what Hrungnir had done. Thor had used the steel mills of the Midgard city of Pittsburgh to forge his protection, and he wondered where Hrungnir had obtained his.

But there was no time to speculate, for Hrungnir now ran toward Thor with his enchanted club ready to strike with his left hand. Barely able to stand, Thor found himself incapable of dodging the blow in time, so instead he raised his right arm and managed to catch the giant's arm in mid-swing just as he had caught the club earlier.

Angry, Hrungnir pushed with all his considerable, armor-enhanced strength. But Thor dropped his hammer and raised his left arm to join his right.

He would not yield. He thought of Frigga, trapped in that keep solely because she fought to protect the children of Asgard.

And so he gathered all his strength and pushed back.

For a time—neither Thor nor Hrungnir would later be able to say for sure how long it was—Thor pushed with both his strong hands against Hrungnir's enchanted left arm.

But then Hrungnir recalled that he had another arm.

The giant's fist struck Thor's chest with the impact of a thousand blows, and Thor stumbled into a crouch to try to catch his breath. Though it meant loosening his grip upon Hrungnir's arm, the crouch served also as a dodge, and the club flew harmlessly over his head. What's more, the sudden-ness of the action caused Hrungnir's arm to fly free faster than expected, and he lost his grip on the club. The weapon flew aside to land in the snow.

Thor knew he had to keep Hrungnir from retrieving the club, but that proved an unnecessary thought, as the giant evinced no interest in the weapon. Instead, Hrungnir grabbed Thor's arms at the wrists and pushed his arms downward into his chest, forcing him to stay in a crouching position.

With all his might, Thor tried to exert similar force, but it was for naught. He felt his arms start to crumple, his own body unable to straighten up from the sheer power attempting to crush him now.

"Do you feel it, Thor? The power that will ultimately destroy you? You may believe it to be the magick of my armor, but it is far more than that. It is my impatience with you Asgardians and your arrogance and your preening. It is my indignation at Odin's effrontery in making a fool of me in front of my own people. It is my anger at your belief that you are gods when you are nothing but tiny little humans with delusions of grandeur."

"Speak not of delusions, for I have done battle with much worthier foes than Hrungnir the Brawler and lived. I have faced many a frost giant, including those far more powerful than you, such as Ymir and Utgard-Loki. I have faced the god of mischief and the goddess of death. I have faced Surtur and the Midgard Serpent. I have faced the Hulk and the king of the vampires. I have faced the paramour of death and creatures who could destroy the universe with but a thought. I have faced the villains of legend and the tyrants of tomorrow." Thor gathered up every ounce of strength and straightened his knees, lifting Hrungnir from the ground. Hrungnir's face fell, his mouth agape as he felt his feet rise into the air, lofted by Thor's strength. "I have faced all manner of creatures great and small and triumphed, Hrungnir. And while I grant that one of those foes may some-day be the one that brings me down, I say now that today is *not* that day! The one who defeats me will *never* be the likes of you!"

With that, Thor threw Hrungnir aside.

Even as the giant landed in the snow with a most resounding crash, Thor felt his own knees buckle once again. Every muscle in his body cried out to rest, but he could not heed their desires, for his foe still was able to rise.

And this time, Hrungnir was not happy. "The likes of *me*? Hah! Never have you faced the likes of me, Thor, for I will not be stopped. Not by your boasts, not by your hammer, not by your fists. Bring me down as many times as you may, I will *always* rise again to destroy you!"

Both combatants lumbered toward each other, now, each moving slowly as if hip-deep in tapioca. For though each dared not show it to his foe, both Thor and Hrungnir were over-whelmed by exhaustion and fatigue from their mighty battle.

But Thor knew that showing weakness would add strength to Hrungnir's desperation, and Hrungnir knew the same held true for Thor. And though Hrungnir had the magic of Loki's armor behind him, in truth he did not entirely rely on it sus-taining itself against attack by Thor, for the giant knew that the source of the magic was not one he could trust. As for Thor, he knew not the source of the magic, only that it was damnably effective, as his aching muscles and weary bones could attest.

Yet still they clashed. Their chests collided, their arms reaching and grasping for purchase.

Thor pushed, and Hrungnir pushed back.

Thor struck, using all the might of his fists, but the armor would not yield.

Hrungnir struck, using all the might Loki's magic had granted his fists, but Thor's will would not yield, even as his mail splintered and his bones cracked.

After trading blows in this manner, Thor had a bit of luck. Their battle had disturbed a great deal of the snow on the ground, and what was normally packed and firm had become loose and slippery. Hrungnir was already unaccustomed to the extra weight of the armor. Keeping to his feet was difficult under the best of circumstances. The loose snow made the circumstances far from ideal, and once again Hrungnir found himself losing his balance and crashing to the ground on his back.

Thor took advantage of this respite to take flight once more. Again, he reached out to the power of the storm. "Winds blow, and rain fall! Thunder strike, and lightning roar! Thor Odinson commands you!"

A massive storm front appeared as if from nothing, the winds kicking the snow up off the ground, making it appear to the naked eye as if it were a blizzard. The low temperatures meant that the rain that would normally ensue instead came down as sleet and hail. Thunder echoed throughout all of Jotunheim, and a massive bolt of lightning came crashing down directly onto the prone form of Hrungnir.

The lightning coursed through the magickal armor, and the giant screamed, both in pain and outrage. He had been assured by Loki that Thor's power would be unable to affect his armor. But the thunder god's attack was considerably more powerful than his earlier thunder strike.

The winds howled louder, the lightning intensified, and the sleet and hail pounded the ground, forcing the other giants to take shelter within the keep for their own protection.

Brow furrowed with concentration, Thor threw more and more power into the storm. Lightning continued to crash into Hrungnir's armor, and the giant screamed louder in pain and shock.

Eventually, it became too much, even for Thor, and he had to stop. However, the storm had, at that point, gained a life of its own and dissipating it would take more effort than Thor had left. He had given the storm his all, and he shakily returned to the ground, the hail and sleet pinging off his helmet.

Still, he could easily withstand the ravages of a storm he had created—though such tumultuous weather was hardly a bother to the frost giants, either. Thor had brought it primarily for the lightning.

But even as his boots touched the snow, Hrungnir got to his feet.

He had a wide grin on his face.

"Is that all you have?"

And then he reared back and punched Thor in the stomach. Too exhausted from his labors, Thor was able only to relax his body and go limp to minimize the damage from the giant's blow.

As he skidded across the snow, Thor realized that the damage was minimized in other ways. He had taken many punches from Hrungnir this day, and this last one was by far the weakest.

Still, while that could be viewed as a victory for Thor, it had come at a high price. The thunder god's ears rang, his vision had gone blurry, his ribs were bruised at best, broken at worst, and he had trouble ordering his thoughts.

Hrungnir moved much more slowly toward his club. "You were wise to try to use the elements to stop me, Thor. Mere strength can no longer defeat me, and the only hope you had was to try to destroy me with your birthright." He picked up the club and laughed bitterly. "But you *failed*! And now it is my turn."

Thor managed to slowly clamber to his feet. He tried to force himself to speak normally, despite the difficulty he was now having simply drawing breath. "Have I failed, Hrungnir? You move more unsteadily. Your words come more slowly."

"But I still move! I still speak! You can barely stand!" He ambled toward Thor, rearing back to swing his club. "And you will not stand for much longer!" Hrungnir's club came careening toward Thor's head in the giant's massive right hand.

Unable to move with any dispatch, Thor instead raised his left arm to deflect the blow.

That proved both wise and unwise. The former because, had the blow struck the thunder god's head, it would likely have decapitated him.

The latter because it shattered his arm.

Again, Thor found himself reminded of Hela's curse. In revenge for defeating Hela in combat and earning the freedom of souls she had claimed as her own, the goddess of death had caused Thor's bones to become as brittle as kindling, something he had discovered the hard way on Midgard during a ferocious battle with the base villains known as the Marauders. Indeed, the pain that coursed through his arm at the splintering of bone now was the worst he'd felt since that day.

Hrungnir threw his head back and laughed. "This club destroyed an oak that has stood for millennia! You are an even bigger fool than I thought to trust that something as pathetic as your arm would stand against it!"

The winds from Thor's storm were still howling, and he focused past the pain that suffused his body in order to grab hold of them once again. Raising his hammer to focus the storm's power, he sent a vortex of wind to surround the giant.

Hrungnir felt the winds buffet him in short order. "What trickery is this?"

But Thor could not answer him, for all of his focus was devoted to increasing power to the mini-twister he was creating around Hrungnir and not collapsing from the agony of his broken bones.

The vortex increased its speed. Hrungnir tried to move forward, but found himself unable to—the force of the wind had become so intense in so short a time that he could not budge.

And then he started to rise.

Helplessly, Hrungnir found himself being raised up by the twister.

Sweat beading on Thor's brow despite the cold, the thunder god urged the vortex to even greater speeds, its force sucking Hrungnir ever upward.

When at last the frost giant was a full league in the air, Thor released the twister. It blew off, and Hrungnir plummeted to the ground.

Where Thor was waiting.

Just before the giant hit the ground he was met with Mjolnir, held by the strong right hand of Thor, who reared back and put everything he had into a swing with the hammer that sent Hrungnir flying across the snowy lands.

He then twirled Mjolnir overhead, gripping it tightly as it carried him to the far-off place where Hrungnir had landed. Falling more than landing, Thor was barely able to keep to his feet, and also barely able to avoid further aggravating his broken left arm.

His left arm now useless, his right arm still holding his hammer, Thor instead used his legs, kicking Hrungnir as hard as he might. Again, the giant flew through the air, and again Thor whirled his hammer and flew after him.

\* \* \*

Back in Hrungnir's keep, all the giants had gathered in the large room where Frigga was held. Except for Thjasse, they all stood at the windows, watching the fight.

"Go Hrungnir!"

"Look at that punch he threw!"

"Thor ain't got a chance!"

"Hey, look, he's gettin' back up!"

"Hrungnir'll just take him down again, don't you worry."

Frigga was concerned that the greater number of giants who had fled to the castle to protect themselves from the storm Thor had called down on Jotunheim would make it harder for her to escape her bonds. But none of the newcomers paid her any mind. Indeed, the only one who even acknowledged her was Thjasse, and all he did was give a quick look to make sure that she was still there.

She had made some progress in getting her gag to slide off her face, but not enough to actually free her mouth sufficiently to cast spells.

"Ha! Lookit, he broke Thor's arm!"

"He's gonna feel *that* in the mornin'!"

"Nah, he ain't, 'cause in the mornin', he'll be dead."

"Yeah, him an' the rest'a Asgard."

"You bet, we'll be ridin' into Asgard and takin' *all* the gods! With Goldfaxi an' that armor, we can't be stopped!"

"Can he even ride the horse with that armor on?"

"If he can't, I wanna ride him!"

"Wait, what's Thor doing?"

Frigga kept rubbing her head against the floor on which she lay, trying to keep moving the gag farther down.

"Wow. I didn't think anybody could punch that hard."

"You obviously ain't never been punched by Thor before."

"I have, and I've never seen him punch anybody as hard as he just hit Hrungnir."

"Geez, I can't even see them anymore!"

Thjasse then left, to Frigga's relief. She had been observing Hrungnir and his band of giants for most of a day now, and Thjasse was the only one besides their leader who had even a modicum of cleverness. With only the imbecilic followers left, Frigga would have an easier time of things.

And then, at last, she managed to lower the gag enough to free her lips.

Slowly, quietly, she began to mutter an incantation. It was one her own mother had taught her millennia ago when she was a child in Vanaheim.

"Be wary, daughter," her mother had warned her. "This is spell only affects those who are already weak-minded. Those who are strong of character and self will not be swayed. In addition, this incantation should only be used sparingly and, most of all, wisely."

"But, Mother," young Frigga had said, "all spells should be used wisely."

That had prompted a happy smile from her mother. "Yes, my sweet girl, exactly. You have learned your lessons well."

Frigga had soon perfected the spell. It had been centuries

since she'd cast it, but she was certain she would be able to wield the incantation again.

She also mourned her inability to impart the same sense of wisdom into Loki with regard to spellcraft that Frigga's mother had imparted to her. Frigga had few regrets in her life. She was the wife of the greatest god who ever lived. She was respected by all of Asgard, and if that regard didn't necessarily extend to all the denizens of the other of the Nine Worlds, at the very least she knew she had the admiration of those whose opinion was worth considering. And she had nothing but pride in her heart and soul for Thor and all that he'd accomplished.

But she regretted deeply that she had been unable to do better with Loki.

She supposed that all mothers had their issues with their children. For all the influence mothers had, sons and daughters were still their own people.

Putting such self-indulgent thoughts aside, she finished the spell and saw that the giants were no longer gaping out the window, but instead staring straight ahead, waiting for Frigga to tell them what to do.

"Untie me," she said.

This, she realized, was a mistake, as all twenty or so of them immediately moved toward her, bumping into and stepping all over each other to try to follow her instruction.

"Stop!" she cried out, then pointed at one of them. "You, untie me."

Silently, the giant she pointed at shuffled over to her and undid her hands.

She shook her wrists out and then stretched her arms, trying to get feeling back into them. This was, she knew, only the first step.

Unfortunately for her next step, Thjasse chose that moment to reenter the room.

"What is going on here?"

Frigga was still too drained from her battle with Hrungnir on the mountain to do aught but maintain the spell on the giants, so she bellowed, "Attack him!"

All the giants started to amble toward Thjasse in a menacing manner, but Hrungnir's lieutenant quickly barked, "Stop, you fools! Do frost giants now take orders from puny Asgardians?"

Most of the giants stopped their forward motion and stood in confusion. Frigga's spell made the weak-minded open to the spellcaster's suggestion, but these giants were already used to taking orders from Hrungnir and Thjasse, and so this new instruction confused them.

And she didn't have the wherewithal to strengthen the spell.

One of the giants remained in her thrall completely, however, and attacked Thjasse.

Or, rather, he tried to. Thjasse countered the giant's clumsy attack, grabbed him, and threw him directly at Frigga.

She tried to run, but the giant was too large, her own legs too short by comparison, and her fatigue too great.

The weight of the now-insensate giant atop her was overwhelming, and Frigga found that she had to focus all her strength on keeping herself from being crushed.

A moment later, the weight was gone, and Frigga saw that Thjasse had removed his erstwhile attacker from atop her. While this was a laudable short-term result, the looks on the faces of the other giants that now all stood over her spoke ill of her long-term prospects.

"Bind her," Thjasse said. "And I would advise not making any further attempts to free yourself, my lady. The only reason I do not kill you is because Hrungnir gave explicit instructions that you were not to be harmed until the battle with Thor was ended. But if you give me reason, I will forego that instruction and kill you myself. Your value was in getting Thor to arrive in Jotunheim alone that he may be thrashed by Hrungnir, and that particular coin has been spent. Do not tempt the fates any further."

Even as one giant held her down, another bound her hands with the same ropes—more tightly this time—and then replaced the gag.

"Uh, Thjasse?" said Frigga's original guard, who was now back at the window.

"What is it?"

"I'm not sure Hrungnir's the one doin' the thrashing."

That got all the giants to return to the window, leaving Frigga once again bound and gagged on the cold floor.

What they saw was Thor continuing to kick Hrungnir's armored form about. They were farther and farther away from the keep, nearing Ymir's Ridge, named after a previous leader of the frost giants.

Thor had been treating Hrungnir as if he were a Midgard soccer ball, refusing to give the frost giant a chance to recover before Thor kicked him again.

But the pain in his left arm and chest was starting to grow roots, and he knew he could not continue on this course for much longer.

His latest kick had brought Hrungnir to the base of Ymir's Ridge, and Thor realized what he needed to do now.

Holding Mjolnir aloft, he commanded the lightning to strike at the ridge.

At his command, the lightning burst forth from the gray skies, shattering the ridge, and sending rock, dirt, and snow cascading downward onto Hrungnir's prone form.

The ground shook further, as the lightning's damage had a cascade effect, sending even more of the ridge collapsing atop Hrungnir. Realizing how bad it was getting, Thor quickly used his hammer to take to the air, letting the avalanche do its work.

But Thor was only able to go a short way before he had to land once again. The thunder god could take very little more, and if the frost giant was not defeated at last by this final blow, Thor was not at all confident that he could continue the fight.

Eventually, the avalanche ran its course. Ymir's Ridge was

broken and jagged, and below it, a massive pile of snow and dirt sat unevenly upon the ground.

The echoes of the ridge's agonized wounding faded from earshot, and soon all was quiet, save for Thor's labored attempts to breathe with his ribs so badly damaged.

Thor stood and waited in the quiet and the stillness. Cold air seared his lungs as he tried and failed to keep breathing without pain.

As the seconds passed, he hoped that victory was his, at last, and Hrungnir had been defeated.

But then the snow started to stir. The dirt began to shift.

And then snow and dirt exploded upward as Hrungnir, his magic armor chipped but intact, leapt to his feet.

Hrungnir himself was exhausted almost to the point of collapse, but he was physically unharmed beyond that. Besides, he had the stone armor to sustain him and keep him upright. And Thor was too far gone to be a worthy foe any longer.

"Look at you, Thor. You can barely stand. Surrender! There is no shame in giving in to your superior. You have given this fight your all, and truly I have never beheld a foe so worthy as you. If you surrender now, I promise that I will deliver you to Hela's embrace with speed and as little pain as possible."

Thor shook his head, an action that made his head swim. "Do you truly believe, Hrungnir, that I would accept so perfidious an offer as that?"

"Perfidious? I treat you as an honorable foe, and you—"

"Honorable? You threaten the very gates of Asgard over an

imagined slight, you kidnap the woman who raised me from a baby, you—"

"Imagined!? Odin made a fool of me!"

"Nay, mighty one, the fates did that. My father merely cast a light upon it. Odin was but travelling alone to be with his thoughts. 'Twas *you* who harassed him and dragooned him into your absurd contest. For that, you have brought havoc down upon Asgard, endangered the lives of dozens of gods and giants both, and for *what*? Vanity? Ego? And then to issue this challenge by toying with the life of the mother of all Asgard, and to change the expectations of battle with your eldritch armor. There is no honor in you, Hrungnir, nor in your actions. And you may rest assured that Thor will *never* surrender! Not even after I draw my last breath will I succumb to the likes of you!"

To punctuate his point, Thor threw his hammer with all the might he could muster—which, to be fair, was far less than usual—directly at Hrungnir.

The giant saw how weak the throw was, and opened his hands as if to catch Mjolnir.

Instead, the hammer slammed into the giant's hands, pushing them back into his chest. The momentum of Thor's throw sent the giant flying back, and while it didn't hurt Hrungnir, it did cause him to crash into the jagged remnants of Ymir's Ridge.

The hammer flew back to Thor, his right hand wrapping around the haft.

Hrungnir struggled to his feet, furious. "So be it, Thor! If you wish to fight until your dying breath, allow me to provide it!"

Thor said nothing. Instead, he twirled Mjolnir in front of him, which sent more and more snow and dirt churning up.

The giant was forced to raise his hands before his face to keep the dirt and snow out of his eyes and nose and mouth.

Every muscle in Thor's body cried out in suffering. Every bone felt as if it were either already shattered or about to be. Every pore felt as if it were on fire.

But still he moved forward, his hammer's twirling continuing to kick up more rocks and snow and dirt. He knew it was naught but an irritant to Hrungnir, yet it was hitting him in the one area in which he was vulnerable: his face, which the armor left exposed. And Thor needed the distraction of the detritus cutting into his face so he could get close.

Once he was near enough, he stopped twirling the hammer, dropped it, and then leapt into the air and punched Hrungnir directly in the nose.

Unprotected as it was, the nose was smashed, blood flying in all directions, even as Hrungnir stumbled backward into the ridge.

Teeth clenched, breaths hissing through them, Thor advanced on Hrungnir, unwilling to give the giant pause. He grabbed the armor at the seam between helm and chestpiece with his right hand, turned, and then threw the giant with all his waning strength back toward the keep.

Never was Thor more grateful for the fact that his power of flight came from Mjolnir rather than himself. That last throw took all Thor had, and he could barely stay upright. He had drawn on every last ounce of strength, and was still on his feet only by dint of the tattered remnants of his will power.

But Mjolnir's enchantment remained undimmed, and so with even the slightest throw, the hammer carried Thor to the ground outside Hrungnir's shabby castle. Thor landed clumsily in front of Hrungnir, even as the giant unsteadily rose to his feet.

To Thor's horror, he saw that Hrungnir's landing point was proximate to where his club had gone flying after Hrungnir had lost his grip on it. The giant now held the weapon in his hands once more.

Hrungnir was grinning. "Did I not tell you, thunder god? Bring me down as many times as you may, I will *always* rise again to destroy you!"

He held the club aloft.

Thor tried to raise his right arm, but he found he had not the strength even for that action.

It seemed that the battle had ended. Thor had nothing left to give, and he would soon be en route to Hela's waiting arms.

Hrungnir swung the club downward toward Thor's head.

And then the club shattered upon impact with Thor's helmet.

At first, both combatants merely stood in shock. Hrungnir and Thor both stared at the tiny, jagged bit of the club's handle that was all that remained in his stone-gauntleted hands.

Finally, Hrungnir spoke in a confused whisper. "How can this be? The club was indestructible!"

"Your use of the past tense serves you well," Thor said with a weak smile of his own. Again he reached out to the spot he had grabbed moments ago, right at the top of the chestpiece.

The stone crumbled in Thor's grip.

"No." The word escaped Hrungnir's lips with a gasp.

Buoyed by his foe's sudden vulnerability, Thor straightened. "It would seem, mighty Hrungnir, that the enchantment upon your armor had a time limit. 'Tis a pity for you that the same cannot be said for Mjolnir's magic. For while your armor's extraordinary gifts came from an inferior source, my hammer's comes from the All-Father himself!" Reaching back, Thor swung the hammer around right at the frost giant's chest. "Behold the eternal power of Mjolnir, hammer of Thor!"

Upon impact, the armor shattered into a thousand pieces.

Even though he dwarfed Thor in size by a considerable margin, Hrungnir now cowered so much that he seemed smaller. Again he whimpered a pathetic "no" as he backed away from the thunder god.

Placing his hammer in its belt loop, Thor advanced upon the giant, gathered what he could of his strength, and punched Hrungnir in the belly.

The giant fell to the snowy ground.

"I have brought you down, Hrungnir. Now, I believe, is when you rise again to destroy me."

Hrungnir did not move.

"I am waiting, Hrungnir! Surely your boast was not an empty one!"

The giant remained still upon the cold ground.

Behind him, Thor heard the sound of heavy footsteps crunching into the snow. Slowly, he turned around to see Thjasse and several other giants exiting the keep.

Thor looked up at Thjasse. "I believe the terms of our bargain were quite clear. I was to meet Hrungnir alone in combat, and the Lady Frigga would be freed. The god of thunder has met those terms, and I would now ask, Thjasse, that you meet yours."

Thjasse raised an eyebrow. "They are not *my* terms, Thor, but Hrungnir's."

"Are you not his lieutenant, sworn to uphold his rule?"

"For the moment, I am, yes."

Thjasse's face was inscrutable, and Thor feared that he would get not the rest and recovery he so desperately needed to mend his battered body, but instead yet more battle.

In an endeavor to forestall it, Thor said, "Consider your next move carefully, Thjasse. Asgard has played fair with Jotunheim. Hrungnir took Odin's wife, an action that would, in the usual course of events, lead to a far stronger response than this. But the All-Father did abide by the terms set out by the base villain who would besmirch the mother of all Asgard—as did I. Do not presume to try the patience of Odin, or me, or the other warriors of Asgard by taking back the word of your leader. Even now, Sif, Balder, and the Warriors Three stand ready with all the soldiers of the Realm Eternal and the Einherjar of Valhalla to storm the battlements of this land should any harm come to Frigga."

"Do they?" Thjasse asked with a smirk.

"Yes. They do."

Still looking at Thor, Thjasse called behind him. "Bring the woman!"

One of the giants dashed back inside.

Thor tried not to let the relief show in his face.

"You have done me a favor today, son of Odin, for Hrungnir's rule was far more predicated on his horse than his skills. Your victory is also a victory for me. That also gives me little reason to abide by any agreements Hrungnir may have made."

The giant returned, bearing a bound-and-gagged Frigga.

Thor tensed, prepared to fly through the air to remove his mother from the giant's grip by force if needed.

"However," Thjasse added quickly, "I also have little reason to begin my own rule with a war against Asgard. Therefore, you and your mother are free to depart Jotunheim in peace." The giant smiled. "After all, *I* currently have no quarrel with you or with Odin—or with the Lady Frigga."

With that, the giant inclined his head in a meager show of respect for Thor, and then backed away from the thunder god, never turning his back on him. "Release her!" he bellowed to the giant who had come out of the keep.

The giant removed the gag and undid the ropes that kept her hands behind her back. Immediately, Frigga ran to her son's side, putting a gentle hand to his right shoulder.

At her touch, Thor all but collapsed, no longer able to stand straight.

"Oh, Thor," she said.

Through clenched teeth, Thor said, "It is as if all the swords in the Nine Worlds are cutting through my left side. I do not believe that I am capable even of flying us home."

"I fear that I am unable to summon the power to bring us home by magickal means."

"Then we shall walk," Thor said.

Frigga shook her head. "You can barely stand, my son. Surely—"

Then they heard the muted clopping of hooves on snow-covered ground, and they both turned to see that Thjasse had brought Goldfaxi out.

"What is this?" Thor asked.

"Hrungnir has little need of his mount at present, and I wish you gone from our lands as quickly as possible. Save for Sleipnir, none may expedite that departure with as much dispatch as Goldfaxi here. Once you return to Asgard, merely pat him once on the rump, and he will return to us on his own."

Thor nodded. "My thanks, Thjasse."

"I do not do this for you, Thor, merely to be rid of you." With that, Thjasse turned and walked away, leaving Frigga to aid Thor in mounting the gold-maned horse. That was a lengthy and painful process, but once they were both astride Goldfaxi—as a horse bred to be ridden by giants, there was plenty of room for both on the steed's back—they began their trek back to Asgard.

# CHAPTER NINE

Once again disguised as a fly, Loki happily flew back to his keep. All in all, it was a generally successful endeavor, and the memory of Hrungnir's righteous indignation and Thor being beaten to within an inch of his life would make the rest of his house arrest far more tolerable.

As a fly, he landed on the bed next to his still-sleeping simulacrum. He then disposed of the doppelgänger and restored his own shape at the same time. Then he "woke up" and stretched and yawned.

Still in his bedclothes, Loki wandered through his home. He noticed that the keep was now clean. The sprites, of course, knew that the eldritch being lying on the bed wasn't truly Loki. No doubt relieved that Loki was actually gone, the sprites had tidied up rather thoroughly. True, he'd told them to perform their function with him present, but he knew they would not be comfortable with it.

So it all worked out for the best. He expected that he would get bored ere long, but that would happen later. For now, he intended to enjoy himself.

He poured himself a flagon of the finest mead and sat in his favorite chair and instructed his scrying pool to show him the recent past—specifically, the beginning of Thor's conflict with Hrungnir.

It began with Thor blathering as he twirled his hammer and flew toward the giant: *"Then stand fast, Hrungnir, for defeat you, I shall! None may harm the personage of the mother of all Asgard without paying the price, and you may rest assured that the cost I exact will be most dear! For Asgard! For Odin! And most of all, for Frigga!"*

Loki almost giggled as he watched Thor crash into Hrungnir, falling violently to the cold ground, while Hrungnir himself had not budged.

Oh, the look on Thor's face! Even better than the look when Mjolnir didn't come back to his hand while fighting the trolls.

*"What sorcery is this?"* Thor cried, and Loki laughed heartily.

"It's *my* sorcery, dear brother! Mine that left you battered and bruised and hurting!"

Loki was about to view it a second time when the wards he kept around his keep signaled that someone was approaching.

And then he sensed the sheer power emanating from that someone, and realized that he was about to have a most unexpected visitor.

It was the work of but a quick spell to alter his bedclothes to that of his usual green raiment, and greet Odin as he entered.

"Well, well, well, I must say this is quite a surprise. Lucky for me, the sprites tidied up."

"Loki," Odin said in an unusually subdued voice. "I would speak with you."

"In my keep? This is—well, peculiar. I believe your usual mode is to summon people to your throne. A sensible method, I must say, as it puts everyone on your terms. After all, who would dare challenge Odin in his very place of power? Your raised throne gives you the high ground in your own territory."

Odin began to pace about the sitting room, not actually facing Loki. "I have come to you for two reasons. One is simply the letter of the law. You are forbidden from leaving your keep, and summoning you to my throne room would facilitate you breaking the terms of your punishment. I could hardly allow myself to be responsible for that."

Loki didn't see how that was much of a concern, since it was Odin's own punishment. What did it matter if he himself violated it? But he said only, "And the second reason?"

"I am not here as the ruler of the Realm Eternal, but as your father."

"And what does my *adoptive* father have to say to me?"

Odin ignored the dig and said, "I am concerned. Your house arrest cannot be pleasant for you. Loki is never happier than when he is out and about and engaging in his petty schemes."

"On the contrary, the petty schemes I miss not at all. It is the complex plots that I regret my inability to complete during this tiresome exile."

"Interesting, that you should mention complex plots. We were the victims of one just recently."

Loki folded his arms. "Oh?" His ignorance was feigned—not very well feigned, but still, he felt he should at least put up the appearance that he had no idea what Odin was talking about.

"After your punishment commenced, I rode out on Sleipnir in disguise. I wished—"

"Yes, I'm aware," Loki said with a dismissive wave.

That got Odin to finally look at Loki, shocked that the trickster would admit to any wrongdoing.

But then Loki smiled. "Mother told me."

Odin let out a sigh. "Of course." He turned away and again started to pace the sitting room, hands behind his back. "While riding, I encountered Hrungnir, the current ruler of the frost giants. He was astride Goldfaxi, his speedy golden-maned mount. He did not know who I was, but he recognized Sleipnir for the fine steed he is. And so Hrungnir did challenge me to a race between our horses."

"I assume Sleipnir won?"

"Naturally. But I did not reveal myself. I simply allowed Hrungnir to believe that he had been defeated by an ordinary old man."

Loki raised an eyebrow. "Oh, he must have been *livid* when he learned it was you."

Again, Odin looked at Loki. "He did learn it was me, yes. And how did you know *that*, my son?"

"Because you wouldn't be boring me to death with this incredibly uninteresting tale if he didn't."

For a second time, Odin was forced to concede to Loki's logic. "When Hrungnir learned I had defeated him, he viewed it as a personal insult—that I did not reveal my true self."

"Obviously," Loki said dryly, "he does not understand your obsessive need to pretend to be someone else. A trait Hrungnir shares with most sensible folk, if it comes to that, Father."

Odin chuckled. "Quoth the shapeshifter. Regardless, he attacked Asgard's very walls, but Thor and the others were able to stop him at the Ida Plain."

"Yes, I did hear the Gjallarhorn. Woke me out of a sound sleep, it did. What a pity I am under house arrest. I could easily have aided my brother."

"That was not necessary, for the frost giants were routed, their leader retreating on his golden steed. But on his way back, he did find Frigga in the mountains."

"And what, pray tell, was Mother doing *there*?" Loki asked angrily. It was a question that had been preying on his mind for quite some time.

"Protecting the children of Asgard at *my* instruction!" Odin snapped. "You covet the throne, Loki, so you would be well to know of *all* the responsibilities that such rule entails! That includes safeguarding *all* of Asgard's citizens! Frigga and Gudrun brought all the children of Asgard to the Vale of Crystal, where they would be safe from Hrungnir regardless of the outcome of his invasion." Odin looked away again, staring now at a bit of statuary on Loki's shelf. "Frigga did stay behind and do battle with Hrungnir to delay him so Gudrun and the children would be safe."

"Is Mother safe?" Loki asked blithely.

"She is now, yes. Hrungnir took her hostage, and bargained

with her life: He would do battle alone with Thor in exchange for Frigga's freedom."

Loki grinned. "Let me guess—my brother flew valiantly into the fray and did thrash the mighty Hrungnir?"

"He attempted to. Hrungnir had been gifted with stone armor that was proof against Thor's greatest blows."

"Impressive."

Odin turned to face his adopted son. "I am well familiar with the frost giants' magick. It is capable of many wonders, but *not* this armor."

Shrugging, Loki said, "Hrungnir has been raiding Nornheim—perhaps the armor is one of Karnilla's tricks, stolen by the giants."

"Perhaps. Its being stolen would explain why it suddenly failed in the midst of battle, allowing Thor his victory."

"That is certainly a good explanation." Loki clapped his hands. "Well, Father, I do appreciate you coming by to fill me in on the latest happenings in Asgard. Please do feel free to stop by any time."

"So you have nothing to say about Hrungnir's campaign against the Realm Eternal?"

"Why would I? I have been trapped here, as Heimdall is my witness."

Odin nodded. "Heimdall does indeed say that he did not spy your departure."

"Do you not trust me, Father?" Loki asked with a grin.

"Do I have reason to, my son?" Odin asked sadly.

They stared at each other for several seconds, and it was Loki this time who broke the gaze, looking away from his father's irritating visage.

"I notice that you have not asked Thor's condition?"

"He did battle and won. His condition does not matter, for he is still alive—were he not, you would have begun your oratory with that particular revelation. Thor is strong, and Asgard has the finest healers in the Nine Worlds. I have no doubt that he will be up and about and annoying me in no time at all."

"It does sadden me, Loki, to see the love that Thor always had for you spit back in his face."

Wandering back to his raised chair, Loki sat in it. Odin wasn't the only one who could claim the high ground in his territory with petitioners, after all.

"Do you recall, Father, the time shortly after Thor's exile on Midgard ended? He was no longer trapped in the body of the crippled healer on a permanent basis, though he did still share his existence. You were frustrated, because Thor had fallen in love with a mortal woman."

"Of course, I recall," Odin said gruffly.

"You kept summoning me to the throne room for advice on how to deal with it. And every time you asked, you referred to him as 'my favorite son.' Over and over, that was what you called him." He shook his head. "I had hoped that your little lesson in humility would last at least until the Blake persona died of old age, but I was not so fortunate. And then you rubbed salt in the wound by *constantly* reminding me that you had a favorite son, and that it was *not* me."

Odin shook his head sadly. "If Loki does doubt the love that the All-Father holds for him, he should think back on all the misery he has caused, all the havoc he has wreaked—and that, with all that, he still lives. And still thrives. Another ruler would *not* have been so considerate."

With that, Odin turned and left.

Loki simply stared at the now-empty sitting room. He grabbed for the flagon of mead, then angrily threw it across the room.

He sighed. The place had been so well cleaned, too.

In truth, he would have been more than happy to grant Hrungnir the stone armor indefinitely. While Loki's original intention was for Hrungnir to use the armor against Asgard's forces on his second attempt to invade, donning it to thrash Thor suited him just fine.

Until he saw *who* the hostage was that had secured Thor's solitary flight to Jotunheim.

Loki would have been more than happy to see Hrungnir make Odin's life miserable. If he thrashed Balder or Sif or the Warriors Three, all the better. If Heimdall was violently removed from the Bifrost by a blow from Hrungnir's club, Loki would shed not a tear. And he certainly had no issue with Thor being beaten within an inch of his life.

But Hrungnir saw fit to kidnap Loki's mother. That was not something Loki would easily forgive—or forget.

He could not help Frigga directly, for she would know of

it. While there were others in the Nine Worlds from whom Loki could disguise his spellcraft, he could not do so from the woman who taught him. And if he moved to aid his mother by magickal means, she would not only be aware of his efforts, but castigate him for it. She would, he knew, insist that he aid Thor rather than herself.

It was the selflessness that he loved about her, and that frustrated him no end.

And so he did as he knew Frigga would ask, and aided Thor by putting a limit on the enchantment. After a time, the armor and the club both would revert to simple stone, easily shattered by Thor's might.

Best of all, the time limit was such that there was still plenty of time for Hrungnir to put quite the beating on his *dear* brother.

Speaking of which . . .

Loki cast two quick spells, one of which restored his mead to its flagon and his side, the other of which started the scrying pool going again. With mead in his belly and a song in his heart, he watched again as Thor crashed into Hrungnir and fell insensate to the ground.

"*What sorcery is this?*"

Elsewhere within Asgard's fabled walls, Thor lay in bed.

Every single part of his body hurt, though it was as nothing compared to how he felt toward the end of the battle with Hrungnir.

Nonetheless, he had won the day. Goldfaxi returned him and Frigga to Asgard's borders and then galloped back to Jotunheim. Sif and the others had been waiting for him, and she and Balder brought him immediately to the healers, while the Warriors Three escorted the Lady Frigga back to her home to recover from her own ordeal. Harokin and the Einherjar returned to Valhalla, disappointed.

A knock at his door, and Thor looked up to see Sif entering with a pitcher of water.

"Ho, Sif! It is good to gaze upon your lovely visage!"

Smiling, Sif said, "Would that I could say the same, but your visage has seen better days."

His left arm immobilized in a sling, Thor moved his right hand to his face, which was covered in cuts and bruises. "Indeed. Your courage in facing me in this state speaks well of you."

Sif laughed, and Thor tried to, only to wince.

"I am sorry, Thor," Sif said quickly.

"Nay, apologize not, fair Sif. When I was a mortal healer, I did often say that laughter was the best medicine. And the pain does, at least, remind me that I still live."

"You have won a great victory today, Thor. Hrungnir's brutality will darken the land no more because of you." As she spoke, Sif poured some of the water into a mug. "The healers also say you need to drink many fluids."

"Another bit of advice I oft gave in my time as one." Thor smiled and took the mug, gulping the water heartily. "So what news is there from Jotunheim?"

"None of Hrungnir, that is for sure. It is said that Thjasse now rules the frost giants."

Thor nodded gravely. "They bear watching. Thjasse is clever, far more so than most giants—including Hrungnir, who was no fool."

Before Sif could say anything, Balder's voice came from the hall. "Ho, the house!"

"Balder!" Thor grinned with glee. To have not one, but two of his dearest friends visit filled his heart with unbridled joy.

The white-haired god entered, holding a burlap sack. "Idunn left these at your doorstep. It seems it's your time to receive the golden apples."

"They will be gratefully received," Thor said.

Balder dropped the sack by the bed and pulled out one of the golden apples of immortality and handed it to the thunder god.

As Thor did bite gingerly down on it—his jaw was quite sore, and his teeth ached—Balder said, "I have just come from Odin. The All-Father is consumed by affairs of state, but he promises to visit this even."

"Thank you, my friend."

Smiling conspiratorially, Balder said, "One of those duties is to talk down Harokin. He wanted to lead the Einherjar across the mountains to Jotunheim as soon as he saw you and Frigga ride home."

"Harokin is a good man," Thor said. "And I would feel as he, were our positions reversed."

"There is also a rumor," Balder added, "that the All-Father did visit Loki's keep."

Sif frowned. "Why would he do that?"

"I do not know."

"I do," Thor said quietly. "Hrungnir's route to invade Asgard was the same as that used by Baugi and his troll horde. More to the point, Hrungnir's armor did stink of Loki's magick."

Shaking her head, Sif said, "But Heimdall told me that Loki never left his keep."

"Even your sharp-eyed brother may be fooled if the trickster is determined enough."

"Perhaps." Sif did not seem convinced.

Balder shrugged. "Regardless, Odin will speak with him."

Thor nodded. "Would that I could be a fly on the wall for that discussion."

"Well," Balder said with a grin, "you *were* a frog once. Perhaps you can become one again."

Thor winced at the memory of one of Loki's more bizarre jests.

A booming voice came from the hall. "Frogs? Don't care much for 'em, though their legs can be quite tasty!"

Sif and Balder exchanged glances. "A voice that could shatter glass speaking of food," she said.

He nodded. "It must be Volstagg."

Sure enough, Volstagg squeezed his frame through the doorway, followed quickly by Fandral and Hogun. "Aye, 'tis the Lion of Asgard himself, bearing gifts!"

Volstagg was carrying a tray about half-filled with food. Behind him, Fandral said, "One of those gifts being a headache from the Lion's braying voice."

160

Thor chuckled and asked, "What bring you, my dear friends?"

"It is customary for a hero to return home from battle to a feast! Your injuries have delayed that, but Thor should wait for no feast—not when the feast can be brought to him!"

Peering at the collection of sweet meats and fruits, Thor said, "It seems more of a sampling than a feast."

Hogun glowered at his friend. "That is because Volstagg felt the need to test everything on the tray."

Volstagg harrumphed. "I could not allow my old friend Thor to eat subpar food. And while Gudrun is usually quite able in the kitchen, she was somewhat shaken by her ordeal in the mountains and the Vale of Crystal, and so I feared her culinary artisanship might have suffered. And so I did make the noble sacrifice of tasting the food, to ensure that Thor would only get Gudrun's best."

Everyone chuckled, and Volstagg set the tray down next to Thor, who gingerly reached for a bunch of grapes with his right hand. Gazing at Fandral, who sat on the bed next to Sif, Thor asked with a grin, "Could you not bring the tray yourselves and keep it from Volstagg's grubby paws?"

"We would sooner again beard the Fenris Wolf in his lair than attempt to separate the voluminous one from a tray containing victuals."

"Fie!" Volstagg went to stand near the window. "I was going to regale Thor with the story of how I singlehandedly slew Thrivaldi the Thrice Mighty, but since my efforts are not appreciated, I shall withhold the tale until I find myself amidst an audience who appreciates it."

Sif stared at Fandral. "Wasn't it *you* who slew Thrivaldi? I do seem to recall you boasting of blinding all six of his heads once."

"Actually, there were nine heads," Fandral said, "and I did only blind some of them."

Hogun stepped forward. "If I may interrupt the boasting for but a moment, I bring tidings of the Lady Frigga."

Thor straightened and swallowed a grape. "How fares my dear mother?"

"She is resting and regaining her strength. While her wounds at the hands of the giant were not as obvious as they were upon the thunder god, they still cut quite deep."

With a grateful nod, Thor said, "She will become strong again. It is a fool who underestimates my mother. Indeed, had she not needed to distract Hrungnir while Gudrun and the children got to safety, but instead fought Hrungnir outright, she might well have triumphed."

Fandral added, "Were it not for Hrungnir's enchanted armor, you would easily have triumphed."

"It matters not," Volstagg said. "True, Thor had a more difficult time of it, but of *course* he was triumphant! How could he not be?"

"I have lost battles before, old friend," Thor said gravely.

"Nonsense! I have told stories only of Thor's valiant triumphs over the foes of Asgard and Midgard. And we all know that Volstagg only tells truthful tales! Like the time I stood fast against Ulfrin the Dragon."

Thor grinned. "And how did the great Volstagg fare against Ulfrin's eldritch breath that saps one's very strength?"

Volstagg frowned. "Eldritch breath? Ulfrin had no such!"

"On the contrary, as a youth I faced Ulfrin, ridden by the Norn Hag herself."

"Hmph. Well, perhaps it was another dragon. What does it matter?"

Balder grinned. "When you are telling the story, friend Volstagg? Not a bit."

Throwing his head back and clutching his ample belly, Volstagg said, "Exactly! At least Balder understands! Now, then, where was I?"

Hogun actually came close to smiling. "Standing fast before Ulfrin the Dragon."

Sif grinned. "Or was it Fafnir the Dragon?"

"Perhaps," Thor added, "it was Fin Fang Foom?"

Dramatically, Volstagg sighed. "Will I never complete this legendary tale?"

"Not," Fandral said, "if at all possible."

Thor grabbed one of the sweetmeats and plunked it into his mouth, chewing carefully with his aching jaw. Though the pain of his wounds had not lessened, the pain in his heart had done so. Sitting here amidst his dearest friends, sharing their food— what little remained—and hearing their laughter rejuvenated Thor in ways that no healer's medicine nor godly stamina could.

And so he rested, and so he laughed, and so he ate and drank, knowing that Asgard was once again safe thanks to him. All he ever wanted was to protect all the peoples of the Nine Worlds. And once he was healed, he would do so again.

So be it . . .

THE END

# EVEN DRAGONS HAVE THEIR ENDINGS

*Read on for a sneak-peek at the
next installment of Marvel's Tales of
Asgard Trilogy from Joe Books.*

The great world tree Yggdrasil sits at the center of the Nine Worlds, linking each world to the other eight.

The most populous of these worlds is Midgard, which its inhabitants refer to as Earth, but the most powerful denizens of the Nine Worlds reside in a different realm: Asgard. These immortals, ruled by the All-Father Odin, possess strength far beyond that of the mortal humans of Midgard.

Thousands of years ago, many Asgardians did cross Bifrost, the rainbow bridge, to Midgard. The peoples of the region in which they arrived saw the mighty immortals as gods, and so worshipped them. Today, some Asgardians still visit Midgard—particularly Thor the Thunderer, wielder of Mjolnir and master of the storms. In the modern age, he is viewed as one of many super heroes who protect humanity from chaos.

But as a youth, centuries before, Thor had been known as the protector of Asgard. The young god took his duties seriously, for he knew that such would be his role as an adult when, as the son of Odin, he would take the throne of Asgard.

Odin knew of Thor's resolve, and so sent him to train with his half-brother, Tyr—the god of warfare. Also a son of Odin,

Tyr was the greatest weapons master in all the Nine Worlds.

When young Thor left for his first lesson in swordplay with Tyr, however, he did not see that another followed: A girl in pigtails stealthily tracked him to the Field of Sigurd.

Upon his arrival, Thor was surprised to see not only the god of war, but also several other young men of Asgard. He recognized only one: a blond youth, like himself, who went by the name of Fandral. All of the boys stood side-by-side, holding wooden swords.

"What deception is this?" the young god asked, confused. "I was told I would be taught by Tyr, yet I see a dozen others here."

Tyr laughed, tugging on his dark mustache. "Did you imagine, Thor, that you are the only boy in Asgard who wishes to learn the craft of swordplay?"

"I suppose not." But Thor had hoped for private lessons from his half-brother.

Tyr tossed Thor a wooden sword of his own. Thor caught it unerringly by the hilt and took his place in the line, right next to Fandral.

"Now then," Tyr said, "the first lesson is how to grip the weapon."

Over the next several weeks, Tyr taught the dozen boys how to hold a sword properly—how to wield it in such a way that it could defend as well as attack, how to assume the proper ready position, and how to grip the sword when striking or parrying. He also paired up the students for practice drills and even had them spar a few times, giving points each time one struck the other with his wooden blade.

The sparring sessions were the only times that anyone was injured. Some of the students did not know their own strength—or their opponents had not taken Tyr's parrying lessons to heart. Of the two boys hurt, one was injured badly enough to no longer be able to fight; the other not badly at all, but his pride was sufficiently wounded that he refused to return.

And each day that Thor went to the field for his lesson, he was followed in secret by the girl in pigtails.

Finally, a month into Thor's training with the god of war, Tyr started the lesson with a lecture.

"Remember that the weapon you wield is only a tool. It is the heart of the one who wields it that will determine victory. All of you will grow up to be warriors of Asgard, and the women and children of the Realm Eternal will be relying upon you to protect them from our many enemies."

It was this statement that finally drove the girl to come out of hiding. She came out from behind the large oak she had been taking refuge behind during the lessons and stood proudly before Tyr and his students, hands defiantly at her hips. "And what," she asked, "if the women prefer to defend themselves?"

Tyr smiled underneath his thick mustache. "At last you have revealed yourself."

Thor gaped. "Sif? Is that you?"

"Yes, Thor, it is I. And I find it strange that you and these other boys are deemed worthy of learning swordplay, but I am not."

Fandral laughed. "If so, girl, you're the only one who finds it so. Women are to be wooed and protected, after all."

Sif walked up to Fandral, and the latter was taken aback to realize that the girl was as tall as he was. "Boy, my name is 'Sif'— not 'girl.'"

"And I am Fandral, not 'boy.' You are Heimdall's sister, are you not?"

"I am."

Tyr interceded. "And she has been spying upon these lessons for quite some time. A true warrior, Sif, does not hide in the shadows. We are not dark elves or trolls who skulk about in darkness."

Turning to face Tyr, Sif said, "I might have asked to join the class, my lord, if I had believed for a moment that you would have consented."

"You know my mind that well, do you?" Tyr asked in an amused tone.

"When Thor first arrived, you asked if he was the only *boy* in Asgard who wished to master the sword." She indicated the dozen boys standing before her. "Your students are all boys."

"Boys who will one day become men who must fight for the Realm Eternal." Tyr shook his head. "I admire your spirit, Sif, but battle is important work—the work of men."

Sif stared up at Tyr's imposing presence. "Can men only do important work?"

"I did not—" Tyr started, but Sif would not let him interrupt her.

"Are the choosers of the slain not doing important work? The Valkyries were hand-picked by Odin for their task—would you consider it unimportant? The golden apples of immortality are kept by a woman, a task that is of sufficient import that we would lose our immortality were it not performed. Women bear the children that replace the warriors who fall in battle. Without them, Asgard would be empty. They who control our very destiny are women. I challenge you, Lord Tyr, to go to the Norns and tell them that the work they do is unimportant."

Tyr threw his head back and laughed. "Very well, little girl, you have made your point."

"Then I may join the class?"

"Of course not."

Thor stepped forward. "Why ever not, Lord Tyr?"

"Little Sif is a beautiful and wise girl—it would not do for her to injure herself."

Sif smiled. "I would worry more about my opponents."

"Nonetheless," Tyr said, "it is my class, and my rules."

"I have been observing your class since Thor joined it," Sif said, "and I have learned a great deal. I believe that I can defeat any of these boys in combat."

Fandral barked a laugh. "I sincerely doubt *that*, little girl. You may be able to make an argument, but that will do you little good in a battle of blades."

"More good than your boasting will, little boy," Sif said.

Tyr rubbed his chin. "Very well. Sif, you shall spar with Fandral. Best three touches out of five."

Fandral whirled on Tyr. "Why not first strike?"

Before Tyr could answer, Sif did so, quoting a past lesson: "Fortune may favor even the poorest warrior with a lucky shot."

"Indeed." Tyr spoke with respect, for the first time thinking that some of his words may well have been absorbed by the pigtailed girl.

Tyr grabbed one of the wooden swords and tossed it toward Sif, who caught it as unerringly as Thor had a month earlier.

Within a moment, the nine students and Tyr had formed a circle around Fandral and Sif, who faced each other. Each of them held their sword in a proper defensive position: blade pointed upward, ready to protect any part of the upper body.

Fandral moved around Sif, who moved only to face Fandral at all times.

The boy grinned.

The girl did not.

Around them, most of the boys cheered Fandral on.

"Get her!"

"Hurry up and beat her, Fandral!"

"We'll never get back to classes at this rate! Thrash her!"

"Go, Fandral!"

"Beat the silly girl and get on with it!"

The one exception was Thor. Given his fellows' jeers, he decided to keep his peace. Though he bore Fandral no ill will, he was hoping for Sif's victory, for he did not share the belief held by his half-brother and the other boys about a girl's place. Tyr, he felt, should welcome Sif into the class with open arms. After all, being a boy hadn't stopped two of the students from washing out of the class. Why not give a girl a chance? But then, Thor had been raised by Odin's wife, Frigga, and none would call *her* weak; if she presented a lesser aspect than Odin, it was only because everyone presented such an aspect when compared to the All-Father.

But Thor dared not say any of this aloud, knowing that it would only incur Tyr's wrath.

Eventually, Fandral's impatience cost him. After moving around Sif for the better part of a minute, he finally made the first move, an obvious swing that Sif parried easily.

They traded blows for several seconds—Fandral always attacking, Sif effortlessly parrying.

Realizing that Sif had been paying at least minimal attention to Tyr's lessons, Fandral redoubled his focus. He did several double and triple strikes, engaging in more complex maneuvers worthy of a proper opponent, which he belatedly was realizing that Sif most assuredly was.

Sif parried every strike.

Now Fandral grew frustrated and became more aggressive—so much so that he left his right side open with a two-handed left swing. Sif ducked that blow and simultaneously slid her blade sharply upward to touch the tip of her wooden sword to his ribs.

Tyr nodded. "One point for Sif."

Only then did Sif allow herself to smile.

As they returned to ready position, Fandral took a very deep breath through his nose and let it out through his mouth. It was a technique Tyr had taught them to keep control of themselves.

"Begin," Tyr said, and this time Fandral did not bother to circle, but attacked immediately.

Fandral's assault caught Sif off-guard and she was unable to parry his second strike, his blade touching her hip.

"One point for each," Tyr said.

As they started their third round, Sif finally pressed the attack on Fandral. He had shown a tendency to raise his sword overhead far more than was necessary, leaving himself vulnerable to low swings. So she waited for an opening, making sure to aim high in her initial attacks before switching to a low swing that caught Fandral completely unprepared.

"Two points for Sif, one point for Fandral."

To his credit, Fandral was more careful in the fourth round. Sif remained aggressive, but Fandral's defenses improved.

At one point, Sif slipped on some pebbles on the ground and barely managed to get her sword up in time as Fandral tried to take advantage. But as she tried to right herself, she fell again, and Fandral easily touched her leg with his sword.

"Two points each."

Thor stepped forward. "That was hardly fair, my lord! Sif slipped!"

"I wonder, half brother, if you did battle against a troll or a frost giant and did say to him, 'Wait! I slipped on a pebble and must right myself before we continue our battle'—would come to a good end for you?"

Sif said, "Thank you, Thor, but I accept the loss of the point.

Life is seldom fair—if it were, I would not need to indulge in this charade to join the class."

Tyr nodded. "This shall be the final round. Whoever scores the point will win."

The opponents once again circled each other. Fandral had taken Sif's measure, and found her to be far more skilled than he would have imagined. Sif had taken Fandral's measure, and found him to be intelligent and adaptable. It was no wonder that Tyr had put him up against her—Fandral was clearly the finest of his students.

For several seconds, they dueled tentatively. Fandral struck; Sif parried. They circled again. Sif struck; Fandral parried. And again they circled.

As time went on, the fight grew more aggressive. The final round lasted twice as long as any of the others had, with neither combatant able to gain an edge.

And then it was Fandral's turn to slip on rough ground, and Sif wasted no time in pressing her advantage, slipping her blade under his to strike on his shin.

Tyr, though, said nothing.

"That wasn't fair!" one of the boys cried.

"He slipped!"

"She can't win on a stupid technicality."

Thor whirled on the last boy. "I wonder, Egil, if you did battle against a frost giant or a dragon and did say to it, 'Wait! I slipped on a pebble and must right myself before our battle continues,'—would such a battle end well for you?"

"That isn't funny, Thor."

Before Thor could reply, Tyr said, "No, it is not." He folded his arms. "But he is correct. Were I to deny Sif her victory, I must also take away Fandral's second point. Therefore I must grant victory—and ingress into the sword class—to Sif."

"Huzzah!" Thor cried, and Fandral also cheered from his prone position.

"Thank you, Thor." Sif then reached out a hand to help Fandral up; the blond boy accepted. "I am surprised to hear your approbation, Fandral."

"Do not be, fair Sif, for even had I been victorious, I would have argued for your inclusion in Lord Tyr's lessons. Asgard would be poorly defended indeed if it did not utilize your skill with the blade."

Thor put a hand on Sif's shoulder, next to one of her dangling pigtails. "As Fandral says, so say I. Welcome, Sif, to our sword class."

"Thank you both." Then she bowed to Tyr. "And thank *you*, Lord Tyr."

"Do not thank me yet, young Sif, for you will either become one of the finest swordsmen—or rather, swordswomen—in the Nine Worlds, or you will return to your home ashamed and without honor."

"I have never gone home ashamed, my lord," Sif said. "Pray you, begin today's lesson."

"I would say," Thor said with a smile, "that the first lesson

176

has already begun. We have all learned that a girl may best a boy with a blade."

"Perhaps," Tyr said. "But it is yet to be determined if a woman may do the same to a man."

# ACKNOWLEDGMENTS

The number of people who deserve thanks for this book are legion, and I hope I manage to get all of them in. I will start with the folks at Joe Books and Readhead Books: Robert Simpson (who first approached me with this), Adam Fortier, Stephanie Alouche, Amy Weingartner, and especially my noble editor Rob Tokar.

Huge thanks, as always, to my amazing agent Lucienne Diver, who kept the paperwork mills grinding and more than earned her commission.

Of course, this trilogy owes a ton to the comic books featuring the various Asgardians that Marvel has published since 1962, and while I don't have the space to thank *all* the creators of those comics, I want to single out a few. First off, Stan Lee, Larry Lieber, Jack Kirby, and Joe Sinnott, who created this incarnation of Thor and his chums in *Journey Into Mystery* Volume 1 #83. Secondly, Lee, Kirby, and G. Bell, for producing "The Invasion of Asgard," a backup story in *JIM* #101, which inspired this novel's prelude. Thirdly, and most especially, the great Walt Simonson, whose run on *Thor* from 1983 to 1987 (as well as the *Balder the Brave* miniseries), aided and abetted by Sal Buscema and John Workman Jr., is pretty much the text, chapter, and verse of "definitive." In addition, I must give thanks and praise to the following excellent creators whose work was particularly influential on this trilogy: Pierce Askegren, Joe Barney, John Buscema, Kurt Busiek, Tom DeFalco, Ron Frenz, Michael Jan Friedman, Gary Friedrich, Mark Gruenwald, Kathryn Immonen, Pepe Larraz, John Lewandowski, Ralph Macchio, George Pérez, Keith Pollard, Valerio Schiti, Marie Severin, Roger Stern, Roy Thomas, Charles Vess, Len Wein, Bill Willingham, and Alan Zelenetz.

Also, while these novels are not part of the Marvel Cinematic Universe, I cannot deny the influence of the portrayals of the characters in the Marvel movies *Thor, Marvel's The Avengers, Thor: The Dark World,* and *Avengers: Age of Ultron* (nor would I wish to deny it, as they were all superb), and so I must thank actors Chris Hemsworth, Tom Hiddleston, Sir Anthony Hopkins, Rene Russo, Idris Elba, Ray Stevenson, Zachary Levi, Joshua Dallas, Tadanobu Asano, and especially Jaimie Alexander (who is the perfect Sif), as well as screenwriters Christopher Markus, Stephen McFeely, Ashley Edward Miller, Don Payne, Zak Penn, Mark Protosevich, Robert Rodat, Zack Stentz, J. Michael Straczynski, Joss Whedon, and Christopher Yost.

Also one can't write anything about the Norse gods without acknowledging the work of the great Snorri Sturluson, without whom we wouldn't know jack about the Aesir. In particular I made use of the *Skáldskaparmal,* which has the original story of Hrungnir's challenge of Odin and battle with Thor.

## Acknowledgments

Thanks to my noble first reader, the mighty GraceAnne Andreassi DeCandido (a.k.a. The Mom). And thanks to Wrenn Simms, Dale Mazur, Meredith Peruzzi, Tina Randleman, and especially Robert Greenberger for general wonderfulness, as well as the various furred folks in my life, Kaylee, Louie, Elsa, and the dearly departed Scooter.

# ABOUT THE AUTHOR

Keith R.A. DeCandido has a long history with Marvel characters in prose. From 1994 to 2000, Boulevard Books published a range of more than 50 Marvel novels and short-story anthologies, for which Keith served as the editorial director. Keith also contributed to the line on the writing side, penning short stories for the anthologies *The Ultimate Spider-Man*, *The Ultimate Silver Surfer*, *Untold Tales of Spider-Man*, *The Ultimate Hulk*, and *X-Men Legends*, and also collaborating with José R. Nieto on the novel *Spider-Man: Venom's Wrath*. In 2005, Keith wrote another Spidey novel, this one a solo book for Simon & Schuster entitled *Down These Mean Streets*.

This also isn't Keith's first foray into Norse myth, as he's written a cycle of urban fantasy stories set in Key West, Florida, featuring a young woman named Cassie Zukav who is a Dís, one of the fate goddesses, and has encounters in that island town with many folks from the Norse pantheon (including Thor, Loki, and Odin). Those stories can be found in the online zine *Buzzy Mag*; the anthologies *Apocalypse 13*, *Bad-Ass Faeries: It's Elemental*, *Out of Tune*, *Tales from the House Band* Volumes 1 & 2, and *Urban Nightmares*; and the short-story collections *Ragnarok and Roll: Tales of Cassie Zukav, Weirdness Magnet* and *Without a License: The Fantastic Worlds of Keith R.A. DeCandido.*

Keith's other work includes bunches of other tie-in fiction based on TV shows (*Star Trek, Supernatural, Doctor Who, Sleepy Hollow*), games (*World of Warcraft, Dungeons & Dragons, Star-Craft, Command and Conquer*), and films (*Serenity, Resident Evil, Cars*), as well as original fiction, most notably the "Precinct" series of high fantasy police procedurals that includes five novels (*Dragon Precinct, Unicorn Precinct, Goblin Precinct, Gryphon Precinct,* and the forthcoming *Mermaid Precinct*) and more than a dozen short stories. Some of his other recent work includes the *Stargate SG-1* novel *Kali's Wrath,* the *Star Trek* coffee-table book *The Klingon Art of War,* the *Sleepy Hollow* novel *Children of the Revolution,* the *Heroes Reborn* novella *Save the Cheerleader, Destroy the World,* and short stories in the anthologies *The X-Files: Trust No One, V-Wars: Night Terrors, With Great Power,* and *The Side of Good/The Side of Evil.*

Keith is also a freelance editor (working for clients both corporate and personal), a veteran anthologist, a professional musician (currently with the parody band Boogie Knights, one of whose songs is called "Ragnarok"), a second-degree black belt in karate (in which he both trains and teaches), a rabid fan of the New York Yankees, and probably some other stuff that he can't remember due to the lack of sleep. He lives in New York City with several folks both bipedal and quadrupedal. Find out less at his hopelessly out-of-date web site at DeCandido.net, which is the gateway to his entire online footprint.